Death of a Cantankerous Caretaker

By

Gretel Hallett

For the ladies at my yoga class: you know who you are!

I hope you enjoy this! Best wishes Gretel Hallett

Note to readers: Some names have been changed to protect the (probably not) innocent, but the village is real, and could be located with a little detection.

This story started because I was annoyed with the caretaker of the hall where we have our weekly yoga class, and said that if we were living in an Agatha Christie novel, he would have been bumped off by now. Someone said I should write that novel, and voila!

Cover art with very many thanks to Lorrie Tallis, an excellent photographer, photo-shop manipulator, and good friend.
https://lorrie.myportfolio.com

The reference to 'Wonky Chomps' is for Etta.

'There is no detective in England equal to a spinster lady of uncertain age with plenty of time on her hands.'

('Murder at the Vicarage', by Agatha Christie)

CONTENTS

WHAT ACTUALLY HAPPENED: TREVOR IS THE ARCHITECT OF HIS OWN DOOM

Tudlinghall is a village of some two thousand souls in a middle of a large rural county. It is a generally friendly village where everyone knows what everyone else is doing, often before they've even thought of doing it. The village is home to Miss Leonie Walsh, spinster of this Parish and retired police officer, who lives with her retired police dog, Truncheon. Miss Walsh is just one of the many spinsters who have chosen Tudlinghall to be their retirement home as it is a well-equipped village within easy distance of a busy and popular market town, and the county's capital city. Tudlinghall is a popular commuter village for the same reason. Truncheon is a very handsome German Shepherd who is a Very Good Boy; he served his ten years in the Police very faithfully and well, and on retiring was adopted by Miss Walsh.

At the time Miss Walsh moved there the village had; a doctors' surgery, a dentist, several general stores, a bakery, a vibrant pub, two petrol station garages, and a place of worship for no less than five of the sects which had schismed from the Church of England at some point in the past. There were also two Church of England Churches, which would actually have been Catholic churches when they were built, but which had been assimilated into the new Protestant religion after Henry VIII solved his marital problems by inventing a version of Christianity which suited him better.

Despite its benign appearance, Tudlinghall is a place where surprisingly dark things happen behind closed doors; but also a village where crimes are always solved, and those responsible are always brought to justice: often by Miss Walsh. Although retired from the police force, her detective instincts had never left her, and she still had a few sympathetic contacts in local police stations prepared to pass on the information she needed to solve the crimes they had been unfortunately unable to.

Miss Walsh was quite a leading light in Tudlinghall; Chair of the Parish Council, Chair of the Women's Institute, Brown Owl of the First Tudlinghall Brownies, Organiser of the weekly 'Knit and (k)natter' group, she listened to children reading at the primary school, organised the flower and cleaning rotas at All Saints Church, edited the parish magazine

Village News and delivered it to the volunteers to take round all the houses in the village, sang in the church choir, kept all the footpaths open by walking them once a month, and was a founder member of the Community Car Scheme. She was also a keen member of the 'Yoga for Beginners' class, held once a week at the Memorial Hall, known to its members as 'Yoga for Geriatrics' given the average age of the participants.

Our story starts one Autumn morning, when Miss Walsh took Truncheon out for his early morning walkies.

'I'm setting my watch for an hour, Trunch,' she said, 'I've got to be back in time for a 9am Community Car pick-up, but we'll get another walk in later for you, I promise.'

They headed out of the front door into a wall of fog. 'Ah, Autumn, Season of mists and mellow fruitfulness, Trunch. Although this is more like a pea-souper than a nice genteel mist.'

Truncheon didn't bother replying; his attention was on all the new smells which had been added since his last walkies. This was a daily newspaper of events down at his level; cats, foxes, pheasants, and deer had all left their calling cards at varying levels of pungency, but most interesting were the olfactory additions by all the other neighbourhood dogs. Truncheon added his own most up-to-date information as often as required as they walked around the lanes, and then made their way towards the playing field.

The fog really was dense that morning; not for the first time that Autumn. There had been several mornings like this, and it certainly added a different dimension to the otherwise very familiar landscape. Miss Walsh rather enjoyed foggy mornings, although they were far less frequent than in her distant youth.

'You know what, Trunch,' she continued, 'I can remember fogs so dense that cars would just appear as if they'd materialised right in front of me, and disappear just as quickly. We hardly ever get fogs like that these days, although I think this one is close.'

Truncheon remained unimpressed. Fog, sunshine, rain; nothing interfered with his enjoyment of walkies, or his total focus on the smells to either side of the footpath. They were his Social Media Feed, and he was scrolling.

Together they progressed slowly up the road as there were just so many things for Truncheon to sniff, but finally they made their way through the gateway of the Social Club. Cars had indeed appeared quite suddenly out of the fog on the road running past the Memorial Hall car-park; the sound of their engines was somewhat muted by the fog, and Miss Walsh had had to be extra vigilant to avoid stepping out in front of one. Somewhere a diesel engine was rumbling, there were several cars already in the car-park, and a light on in the bar, which hardly penetrated the fog at all. They walked around to the left, and Miss Walsh threw a ball for Trunch to chase off into the fog. He disappeared after it at full pelt, and she set off much more sedately in the same direction.

There was the sound of barking in the distance, so she whistled for Truncheon to return, and to her surprise a large Golden Retriever she'd never seen before appeared and dropped a spongy dog ball at her feet. The dog had clearly escaped from its owner, as its lead was trailing along the ground behind it, but didn't seem to be preventing the dog running full tilt. Before she had time to react, Truncheon ran in between her and the strange dog, snatched up the ball and fled, the other dog in hot pursuit. She couldn't see either of the dogs through the fog, but their superior senses easily located her, and the strange dog reappeared suddenly with a tennis ball in its mouth this time. It dropped the ball at her feet, looking up at her in the hope she would throw it, and dancing on its front paws. Then Truncheon materialised out of the fog, snatched the ball up and ran away very fast, with the other dog in joyful pursuit, barking loudly.

When she stopped laughing, Miss Walsh whistled Truncheon, and this time he appeared first without the ball in his mouth. She held her hand down by her side to indicate that he should come and sit down, which he did. The other dog ran out of the fog again, and pranced about in front of Truncheon, clearly inviting him to come and play, but Trunch just looked nobly straight ahead, and waited to be released. Somehow between them, the two dogs had lost both the balls.

'That's not like you, Trunch,' Miss Walsh said, 'You never lose your ball!'

Trunch looked embarrassed.

'Bella? Bella!' A woman's voice could be heard calling, but the Goldie paid no attention whatsoever.

'Over here!' Miss Walsh called as loudly as she could, and then said, 'Sit!' to the dog, which looked very surprised, but sat down, allowing her to catch hold of its lead and await its owner.

A figure emerged from the dense fog, a woman of similar age to Miss Walsh, bundled up against the weather, it was hard to see much of her under a hood, scarf, padded coat, and knee-length boots.

'Oh, there you are!' she said, and took the lead Miss Walsh held out to her. 'Thank you ever so, I couldn't see a thing in all this fog, and she won't come when I call if there's another dog about.'

'You're welcome,' Miss Walsh said, and couldn't resist showing off a bit by saying, 'Heel!' to Truncheon, and he obediently trotted at her side.

The Goldie was jumping up at the woman and biting the lead, as well as lunging towards Truncheon.

'All right! All right!' the other woman said, as she bent down to unclip the dog's lead. She took a tennis ball out of her pocket and threw it hard with a deft sideways flick of her wrist.

'That's a good strong throw,' Miss Walsh said admiringly. 'I teach my Brownies how to throw like that; other-wise they just throw underarm, and the ball loops up in the air and hardly goes any distance.'

The Goldie came bounding back with a different coloured tennis ball, and Miss Walsh wondered what had happened to the one that had just been thrown; presumably the dog was finding balls which had been lost by previous dog walkers.

'That's not our ball, Bella!' the other woman said, 'Oh never mind,' and she picked it up and threw it again, with another deft flick of her wrist.

The Goldie hurtled after it, and returned with a short branch in its mouth.

Miss Walsh's smart watch pinged, and she said, 'That's my time up. I have to go, I hope you enjoy the rest of your walk,' and with Trunch still walking sedately at her side, she headed back towards where she hoped the Memorial Hall was – even with a light on, at this distance it was completely lost in the fog. To her surprise, she ended up on the wrong side of the hall, facing the bowls green, but at least she could see the building now that she was this close to it, so she walked along the edge of the building, and emerged back into the car park.

'Well, Trunch,' Miss Walsh said, as they made their way back along the road to their house, 'If she's a new neighbour we don't know much about her except that she's no biologist. Either that or she's very short-sighted.'

Trunch gave her an old-fashioned look. He had noticed Bella's gender quite some time ago; in fact, it was the first thing both of them had established when they met. But he now dismissed the matter as far less important than the fact it was his breakfast time. If he'd been human, he would have shaken his head sadly, but as he was a dog, he merely trotted smartly up their drive and round the back to the kitchen door.

Miss Walsh and Trunch wiped their muddy feet before going back in to the house for their breakfast, and Trunch settled down for a post-prandial nap while his mistress collected everything she needed for her Community Car pick-up.

CHAPTER TWO: AN EMERGENCY AT THE PLAYING FIELD

It was an hour later as she drove along Mill Street to the junction with the main road, that Miss Walsh saw several Police cars approaching at speed from the direction of the city. She pulled out left on to the main road, and drove as slowly as she could past the pub and the Old Vicarage, keeping an eye in her rear-view mirror in case she had to pull over to let them past. The police cars turned off left into Mill Street. A little further on, as she passed the Primary School on her left, a positive convoy of emergency vehicles rushed towards her from the direction of the nearby market town. There were ambulances, fire engines and more police cars. It wasn't possible to see where they went, but the chances were good that it was in the same direction as the other cars.

It was too late for her to turn around and go back to investigate; Mr Powley was waiting to be taken to the main city hospital, and there was no time to ring the Community Car organiser and ask for someone else to collect him. She would just have to find out what on earth was going on as soon as she got back; hopefully there would be personnel on duty from one of the police stations who knew her so that she could get insider information. And hopefully a friendly Detective Inspector would be assigned to the case; in the past some of them had been grateful for her help, and she hoped they would be particularly so as she lived in the village and could give them the inside gen. Of course, it may all be a storm in a tea-cup; a domestic, or a fallen tree, or something which wouldn't require her expertise; but given the response to the call-out, Miss Walsh would have put money on murder at the very least.

Miss Walsh made her pick-up in Trotwood, and was very glad that she hadn't attempted to cancel Mr Powley; he was very grateful indeed at being given a lift to his hospital appointment. He was also very lonely after the death of his wife, and talked all the way there. Miss Walsh had little to do but make the appropriate noises at intervals and concentrate on driving, but she knew that she was providing a valuable service in giving him someone to talk to as well as someone to get him safely and easily to his appointment without having to attempt to get on a bus, or pay a huge amount for a taxi.

Mr Powley's appointment was in the Eye Clinic, so Miss Walsh got him registered as having arrived, and settled him down on a seat in the waiting area. She made sure he knew to listen out for his name being called, and then told him she couldn't stay with him as there wasn't enough room, but that she'd pop back regularly to see if he was finished or not. Then she took herself off to the canteen for a much-needed cup of tea, and made a phone call to a good friend who also lived on West Green.

'Marjorie? It's Leonie.'

'Hello, where are you?'

'At the hospital.'

'Community car?'

'Yes, Eye Clinic.'

'You'll be a while then.'

'Yes, I expect so.'

It says something for Miss Walsh's general state of health that her friends would assume any attendance at the N&N was due to her community service rather than a medical need of her own.

'What can I do for you?'

'Would you be a dear and have a look up and down the road to see what's going on? I saw lots of emergency vehicles headed that way as I left earlier.'

'Oh yes, I did see a lot of blue lights going past,' Marjorie said, 'I'll get my coat on and go and have a nosy. Do you want me to ring back? I haven't quite got the hang of this texting thing yet.'

'Yes, if you would, thank you Marjorie.'

Miss Walsh sat quietly, sipping her tea, and attempting to solve the day's Wordle puzzle. Unlike her friend, she had always embraced new technology and was adept at using the various apps on her regularly updated mobile phone.

It was quite half an hour before Marjorie rang back. In that time, Miss Walsh had been twice to check on Mr Powley, but he was still there, right where she'd left him. She tried asking the woman on Reception how much longer Mr Powley might have to wait, but she wasn't able to say. Clearly the Eye Clinic was living up to its reputation amongst the community car drivers, and running late.

'Are you all right here, Mr Powley?' She asked as she checked on him for the third time.

'Yes, thank you,' he replied, 'They haven't called my name yet, and I've been listening out carefully just like you said.'

'Hopefully it won't be too much longer,' Miss Walsh said reassuringly, 'But I'll stay here with you now, as it's cleared out a bit, and there's some spare seats. If it fills up again, I'll have to go out, but we're all right for now.'

Mr Powley had just gone in for his check-up, when Marjorie rang back.

'Just a mo, Marjorie,' Miss Walsh said, as she rapidly exited the waiting room, and took a seat on the wooden picnic benches outside.

'Ok, I can talk now, what have you got?'

'It's at the Memorial Hall, whatever it is,' Marjorie said, 'Dozens of emergency vehicles, crime scene tape, uniforms everywhere, it's most exciting!'

'Were you able to speak to anyone?'

'No,' Marjorie said regretfully, 'There was a police-lady, or whatever they call them now, guarding the gates, and she just said there was no information at present, but that the hall and playing field couldn't be accessed and would I move along please?'

'At the playing field?' Miss Walsh said thoughtfully, 'I was there this morning with Trunch.'

'Did you see anything?'

'No, it was very foggy, but there was another woman there I hadn't seen before, also walking a dog. I hope she's ok.'

'Oh dear, I hope so too,' Marjorie said, 'I didn't mean to sound so ...'

'No, it's all right, I quite understand,' Miss Walsh said. 'It is exciting when something happens close by, we don't always remember someone may have died.'

'Exactly. So, when will you be back?'

'My client is just in his appointment now, so hopefully within the next hour.'

'Call in for a cup of tea?'

'Yes, thank you, and then I'll go up to the Memorial Hall and hope I recognise someone who can fill me in on what's happening.'

It took longer than she'd hoped to drop Mr Powley off home, and return to Tudlinghall. As Miss Walsh was about to drive off home, a sign for 'Jolleys' made her remember that Truncheon was nearly out of Wonky Chomps, so a diversion to buy him supplies of his favourite treat was a necessity. Then there were several other small items which she could probably have done without for herself, but which she may as well buy now that she was in the vicinity of Morrisons. It was past her lunchtime too, so she had a snack in Morrison's café and reasoned that the longer she gave the first wave of Police to investigate whatever had happened at the Memorial Hall, the more inclined they might be to chat once they had begun to be bored by standing around and diverting traffic away from the site.

She would not admit to herself for one second that this procrastination was nothing to do with the last time she had encountered the police over the Coe case, when she had been torn off a strip by a furious Chief Constable who had no time for amateurs who solved the case after the police had done a superficial job and come to the wrong conclusion. Miss Walsh had held her head very high on that occasion and pointed out that without her investigation, the killer would have remained at large, and the poor woman's would not have received justice for what was a truly terrible death. But the interview with the Chief had left a sore spot on her soul, if she were truthful. Her own career in the police force had been at a time when women police officers were still regarded by their male colleagues as little more than tea-ladies, or reassuring presences if they had to attend a domestic with children present, but were not expected to do any actual policing. Or worse, had been the butt of rough male humour and pranks, which they were expected to tolerate, and even laugh along with.

Miss Walsh had kicked long and hard against the restraints put upon her because of her gender, and had clawed her way up the ladder to Inspector, having been refused admission on to the Detective ladder. But she had only done so by being twice as determined and professional and hard-working as the men around her. She had also accepted jobs in places that were turned down by the men who had applied for promotion at the same time as her; it had been incredibly tough but she had won through, and she was very proud of her service to Her Majesty's Police Force.

She'd known perfectly well that she'd been promoted and posted to inauspicious places in order to get rid of her, but she hadn't cared. Once she was in post, Miss Walsh had been determined to do everything she could to be the firm but fair face of modern policing in the community, and she was perfectly satisfied that she really had done all she could. Her success in post meant she could thumb her nose at those who thought she'd be put off by the roughness of the area, and resign.

They'd managed to finally get completely rid of her to an early retirement on the grounds of redundancy; small police stations were closing all over the country in the latest Government purge, and somehow there just wasn't a role for an Inspector anywhere else.

So, Miss Walsh had taken her early retirement, her redundancy pay-out, and her pension, and bought a small house with a large garden in Tudlinghall. There were former colleagues who did remember her with affection, and were prepared to slip her bits of information on cases they had found themselves stumped over, and her success rate justified the risk they took, but there were also increasing numbers of those who were very hostile towards her and towards any amateurs attempting to tell them their business.

As she drove back over Raddley Moor, Miss Walsh had to hope it was one of those sympathetic colleagues who'd drawn the short straw and was out on the gate redirecting curious traffic. But before she could even get there, she had promised to pay a visit to Marjorie, and so she pulled off West Green into Marjorie's drive.

Marjorie was almost hopping from foot to foot with excitement as she opened the front door, and barely waited for Miss Walsh to lock her car before bursting into voluble speech.

'Oh, there you are! Where have you been? I thought you'd have got here an hour ago! Come in, come in, the kettle's on. Oh sorry about that,' (as her Jack Russell rushed at Miss Walsh's ankles, growling, despite the fact that they had known each other for years), 'Just kick him away, he's such a nuisance! Well, I've got such a lot to tell you …' (her voice trailed off as she dashed back into the kitchen and Miss Walsh heard the kettle start to re-boil).

'Duck!' Miss Walsh said sternly, 'Bed!'

The dog looked around for support, but Marjorie was still in the kitchen, so it succumbed to force majeure and sloped off to its bed.

Miss Walsh was undeniably fond of Marjorie, but allowing small grandchildren to name a dog was not a good idea in her opinion. The grandchildren had been adamant that the dog be called, 'Duck' after one of their favourite CBeebies characters. Marjorie didn't seem to mind bellowing 'Duck, Duck, Duck-ee!' while out on walkies, but it certainly turned some heads when people misheard her. Miss Walsh thought a dog should have a dignified name at least, and naming a dog 'Duck' was the height of stupidity.

Marjorie came backwards into the room pushing the door open and then turning round to reveal a very laden tray of tea apparatus, and snacks.

'Oh, good boy!' she said to Duck, noticing he was in his basket. He gave her an appealing look, but didn't dare to come back out again while Miss Walsh was glaring at him.

'Now, let me tell you all about it,' Marjorie said after all the business of dispensing tea and snacks had been got through to both their satisfaction. Denied the chance of stealing food from the low sitting-room table, Duck was now sulking with his back to the two women; neither of whom noticed, such was their focus on the topic at hand.

Despite Marjorie's diligent attempts, and her own follow-up investigations, Miss Walsh could not find out why the Police were so interested in the Memorial Hall, nor what had happened to completely close the whole site down. She received a telephone call from someone at the main Police Headquarters which told her nothing but that there had been a fatality, and that the hall was closed until investigations were complete. The woman was, she said, telephoning to everyone who had booked the hall out for the next two weeks, just in case it was not possible to re-open the hall for their booking.

However, Miss Walsh was able to say that she had been on the playing field the morning of the alleged fatality, and was asked to give a statement, which she did in person at the nearest police station.

She heard nothing more until she just happened to be watching the local TV news one evening a week after the event, and a photograph of a much younger Trevor Fish, looking uncomfortable in a suit and tie, flashed up on to the screen, and the presenter put on a serious face and voice to announce:

'The quiet village of Tudlinghall, just nine miles away from the studio, has been rocked by the sudden death of a much-loved resident. Trevor Fish lived in Tudlinghall all his life, and after being made redundant by Crane Fruehauf in the nineteen eighties, took on the role as caretaker at the Tudlinghall Social Club. Our chief crime reporter has been to Tudlinghall Social Club to get the latest news.'

The camera cut to the reporter, also looking appropriately serious, and standing outside the Social club. Miss Walsh's attention was completely rivetted on the news item; the whole site which she knew so well looked somehow different when shown on television – it looked more important somehow, as if that slightly glamorous gloss that television confers had been washed across it.

The reporter was standing at the very gates of the social club; had she wanted to, Miss Walsh could have run out through her front door, up the road and seen the reporter live, but she decided not to. By the time she had done so, the news item would be over, and she would miss what they had to say. And there was just a suspicion at the back of her mind that the news item had been pre-recorded, and wasn't actually live, in which case she'd be totally wasting her time.

'I'm here at the Tudlinghall Social club, where the long-serving caretaker, Trevor Fish was found dead a week ago today. Details of the death have just been released by the police, who are appealing for anyone with any information to come forward.'

Miss Walsh huffed to herself; that meant they had no idea what had happened and were hoping someone would come forward and either confess to the murder, or tell them exactly how the accident had happened.

The camera panned out and standing next to the reporter was a woman who was looking very uncomfortable at having a camera pointed at her.

'Mandy Pope worked with Trevor Fish in the bar at the social club for many years. Mandy, are you are able to tell us what happened?'

Mandy had clearly been coached on what she could and couldn't say, and launched into a highly improbable eulogy for her dead colleague.

'Trev was a lovely man, he'd do anything for anyone, he would.'

'What was he like to work with?' the reporter asked.

'Oh, he was ever so hard-working,' Mandy said mendaciously, 'He loved this club, it was his life, and he was never happier than when he was here.'

'And were you the one to find him?'

'No, I didn't, oh poor Trev!' and here Mandy started crying again, and after lingering uncomfortably on her for slightly too long, the camera zoomed in again on the reporter, and then out to his other side where a police officer had apparently just materialised.

'I have here with me Police Constable Jan Rivers. Jan, what happened here? Was it an accident or was Trevor murdered?'

PC Rivers had also been well coached on what she could say. 'We were called to the Tudlinghall Social Club last Friday morning by a dog-walker.'

Miss Walsh took a deep breath. A dog walker? She had been there on that fateful morning, but she had not been the dog walker who called the police. It must have been the other woman – somehow the other woman had found Trevor Fish, and she and Truncheon hadn't! Unless he had been killed after both of them left, and it was somebody else who had found him and called it in?

'Mr Fish was found in a ditch adjoining the property, and his death remains unexplained.'

And here Miss Walsh couldn't help thinking, 'Well I'm afraid it serves him bloody well right.'

Although her callousness may be explained by decades of exposure to villains who thoroughly deserved to die (as well as innocents who didn't), it may be worth reviewing her own relationship with the deceased on this occasion, and hopefully her complete lack of de mortuis nil nisi bonum* will become understandable.

**Literally, 'Of the dead nothing but good is to be said', or as it's probably more commonly known, 'Don't speak ill of the dead'.

CHAPTER FIVE: BASICALLY, TREVOR WAS AN ARSE

Despite the many hours Miss Walsh devoted to her adopted village, her path through Tudlinghall was not strewn with rose petals, and one of the people strewing thorns across her path instead was Mr Trevor Fish, caretaker of the Hall in which she held or attended many of her groups and events. In no universe anywhere would Trevor and Miss Walsh have got along. No matter how many parallel universes you search, they will be perennial enemies; like Tom and Jerry, but without the latter's good-humour and comedy. In fact, he had been so rude and obstructive so often, that Miss Walsh had started the process of moving all her clubs and societies to the Church Rooms next to the Old Vicarage on the main road.

Trevor's refusal to actually do the job he had been employed for was markedly evident when Miss Marsh arrived at the Memorial Hall each Friday morning for the yoga class as he had refused to get to the Hall early and switch the heating on for the class in the cold weather. Rose, the long-suffering yoga teacher, had to get there as early as possible to switch the heating on so that the large space would be slightly less than freezing when the rest of the class arrived. Once the heating was switched on, Rose would locate a large, very tatty, broom and endeavour to sweep up the debris of the previous week's meetings, parties, and get-togethers: Trevor didn't appear to realise that cleaning the hall was anything to do with him. On several occasions there had been a party in the hall at some point prior to the yoga class and the floor was covered in glitter, and streamers, as well as the usual ropes of dust. The ancient broom had to be put to work again, and instead of putting the sweepings in a bin, Rose (encouraged by Miss Walsh) left the large pile of rubbish and dust in the far corner. It was still there a month later. Any attempt by Rose to ask Trevor to actually carry out the work he was employed to do caused a massive grump, and seemed to make things worse rather than better.

Village life in Tudlinghall was vibrant and there were frequent bookings for the Hall, but even though the yoga class met every single Friday at exactly the same time, Trevor would still on occasion double-book the slot. Miss Walsh arrived one notable Friday morning to find the hall full of tables and chairs.

'What on earth is going on?' Miss Walsh asked, staring at all the tables and chairs where there should be yoga mats.

'He's let the hall for a Wake,' Rose said resignedly. 'When I asked him how this could happen given that we have the hall booked every Friday morning at this time, he said he didn't write our booking in the diary!'

'He really is bloody useless!' Miss Walsh said angrily. 'He's double-booked me in the past too! And he once bolted the doors from the inside so I couldn't get in with the key. Last year he even had all the locks changed and didn't tell me, so when I arrived for Brownies, we couldn't get in and he didn't answer his phone when I tried to ring him.'

On another occasion Miss Walsh arrived at the hall before Rose to find a woman in a state of agitation in the car-park. She was wearing sports kit, and Miss Walsh hoped she might be a new recruit, so she approached her to ask if she could help.

'Oh no,' the woman said, 'I'm not here to do yoga, I've booked the hall today for a party, and I'm a bit worried about all these cars here as I'll need all the parking spaces for my guests.'

'Well, we have the hall booked until 10.30am,' Miss Walsh said, 'And most of the group walks here, so I don't know whose cars these are, but they may be overflow from the café and enterprise park opposite? I believe the caretaker is supposed to tell the enterprise park if the hall is booked so that they don't use this carpark for overflow.'

'Oh, I see,' the woman said, 'Well, I don't need the car-park till lunchtime; I was just worried that these cars would be staying here all day.'

'I suggest you find the caretaker and get him to tell the enterprise park that the hall carpark is booked so they can tell their clients to move their cars,' Miss Walsh said, and the woman disappeared in search of Trevor. Miss Walsh shook her head and waited to tell Rose about the latest debacle when she arrived to unlock the hall.

Then there was the fact that every Friday morning, during the one hour of the whole week when the Hall was in use, Trevor would be as noisy as possible in the adjoining Bar area; particularly during the last five minutes of the class when everyone was lying quietly on their mats in Shavasana.

Then Trevor would go into over-drive; crashing, banging, talking loudly, operating machinery, moving barrels, walking past the windows doing something as noisily as possible, or firing up his diesel tractor mower. This was worse in the summer when Rose had the doors open for cooler air; and the ladies in the class did their best to ignore this aural persecution.

What Miss Walsh had found much harder to ignore had been his aggressive attempts to drive them away from the venue during the easing of Lockdowns in 2020. If you recall, in between full lockdowns, everyone was in a kind of limbo, governed by confusing rules which no-one really understood but did their best to comply with. At one point in the year, people were not allowed to fully socialise; cafes, restaurants and other public amenities were still closed, but people were allowed to meet up with no more than six other people in an outdoor location.

Keeping to what she hoped was the letter of the law, Miss Walsh arranged with five other ladies from her yoga class to meet up at the Tudlinghall Social club (weather permitting), and go for a walk, returning to the club to sit outside at the back on some well-spaced picnic benches (one per bench), where they could chat and drink coffee out of flasks.

As far as Miss Walsh could ascertain, this was a harmless enough arrangement in line with the regulations at the time. As the Tudlinghall Social club was run by a charity as an amenity for the people of Tudlinghall village, she could see no reason why anyone would object to their presence once a week for around an hour.

However, object it seemed one person did; and that person was the caretaker, Trevor Fish. The six ladies were sitting at their separate tables, exchanging recipes for banana bread, and recounting their Tales from the Lockdown, when Trevor emerged from the Social Club, and strode towards his tractor. Miss Walsh waved to him, but when he didn't say 'hello', or acknowledge their presence in any way, she turned back to her very pleasant chat with Rose and the other ladies.

Now, the playing field behind the Social Club is very large; it stretches away into the distance, bounded by the grounds of Tudlinghall Grange on one side, and Minor's Garage plus the grounds of a large house on the other. It encompasses full sized football pitches, a cricket crease, and a bowls lawn over an area of flat grass that measures more than five acres. Had Trevor had taken the tractor mower down to the bottom of the field, it would barely have been audible to the ladies on the little patio outside the sports hall.

The grass that stretched right up to the edge of the little patio had already been cut to within an inch of its life. It looked smooth and neat, and certainly not in any need of cutting, particularly as no sporting groups were currently allowed to use it. Although it is a very large field, Trevor decided that the bit which needed cutting the most was the bit right in front of the small patio area where the ladies were sitting, and he fired the tractor up and aimed it straight towards them.

I don't know if you've ever been close to a badly-maintained diesel tractor in full flow? It's very noisy, and very smelly; conversation becomes impossible, and the air quality is significantly reduced, even in the great outdoors. As Trevor manoeuvred the machine closer and closer until he was sweeping right up to the tiny patio, the women were assaulted by exhaust fumes, and deafened by an all-encompassing roar from the engine. Within a short amount of time, they were all coughing, and waving their hands in front of their faces in a vain attempt to clear the smoke away, but it was no use; they were forced to retreat to the other side of the building, their little get-together ruined.

Miss Walsh attempted to catch Trevor's attention to ask him to desist, but he was resolutely not noticing as she strode towards him, and instead turned the tractor-mower in a lazy half circle away from her, making sure that the exhaust pipe was always belching smoke in her direction. It was impossible to make herself heard over the noise of the engine, and undignified to chase him around, so Miss Walsh had to give up and return to where her friends were all packing away and beating a retreat. Had any of them been a few years younger, they would have filmed him and uploaded the outrage onto social media, but women of her generation are not so phone and social-media minded.

As the women congregated despondently outside the front of the social club, Miss Walsh was furious.

'How dare he smoke us out like that? The Social Club is run by a charity for the benefit of the people of the village. It is a public space, and not Trevor's private domain! We are quite within our rights to meet here.'

'How mean-spirited of him too,' Pam said, 'It's been months since we've been able to meet up, and some of us have been alone in our homes, we need this time to reconnect with other people.'

'Yes, we've finally been allowed to meet up,' Rose said, 'And he goes and does this. I've had it with him, I'm looking for another hall for when we can go back to classes again.'

'I'm going to take all my groups elsewhere too,' Miss Walsh said grimly. 'We were only intending to be here for an hour at the most, and he's got the whole of the rest of the day, and indeed the whole of the rest of the week, to do whatever he wants to do with his smelly, noisy, diesel tractor. There was absolutely no need whatsoever to mow that particular bit of grass at that exact moment.'

'If this was an Agatha Christie novel,' Pam said, 'Someone would bump him off!'

They all laughed a little and then Rose, ever the optimist said, 'Well, let's try again next week, shall we?'

And now it seemed that someone agreed with Pam; Trevor was dead, and the amount of police interest indicated to Miss Walsh that the death had not been a natural one. She was itching to find out more, but so far had been kept very much at arm's length by the local constabulary. The constable who had taken her statement had been very frosty and not at all inclined to chat, or give her any information about the direction the enquiry was headed.

CHAPTER SIX: ENTER THE (REAL) DETECTIVES

The usual procedures had been scrupulously adhered to, and all was proceeding along correct lines in the investigation into Trevor Fish's death. As there was no doubt as to his identity, they hadn't needed to call family in to identify him, but the initial report of his untimely demise had been sent to the Coroner who had the final say in whether any further investigation was needed.

PC Jan Rivers and DC Mike Whitaker got on with other matters; there was always another case which needed attention, or paperwork to get up to date and file properly.

The Coroner came back quite quickly to say that she would like reports from the garage into the condition of Trevor Fish's tractor, and a GP report from whichever surgery he was registered with into his state of health. The outcomes of those two reports plus the post-mortem would then enable her to decide whether any further police enquiry was required.

Jan put in a request to the owner of Minor's Garage in Tudlinghall, and to the Tudlinghall Surgery for the information required by the Coroner. The post-mortem report arrived later that day, and DS Branton told his officers to get off home, and be back in early the next day to review their information and decide what to do next.

When they all arrived the following morning, DS Steve Branton opened the batting.

'Right, Jan, Mike, we've got the post-mortem report, which I'll go through with you in a moment. Have you got anything new?'

Jan looked at Mike, who said, 'Nothing new's come in to us, sir. No-one's rung in with anything, no emails or nothing.'

'Ok, run me through it from the beginning. Something might occur to one of us.'

Mike nodded at Jan, and she said, 'Deceased was discovered by a dog walker.'

Branton smiled, 'We really ought to recruit all dog walkers as Specials,' he said, 'They're always finding bodies for us. Details of this dog walker?'

Jan consulted her notes. 'Dog Walker is a Mrs Kylie Cooper, recently moved to Tudlinghall from Braintree. A neighbour told her she could walk her dog around the playing field at the Sports Club. She entered the field around the left of the building, and started to walk around the perimeter. Dog ran ahead and started barking. When she caught up with the dog, it was barking at a tractor which she could see was at an odd angle. When she reached the tractor, it was tipped up in a ditch, and she could see some legs underneath it. She dialled 999.'

'Sensible woman. Anything else from Mrs Cooper?'

'She took the dog home, then returned to the field to await the emergency services.'

'And she lives?'

'Just down the road from the site, on the opposite side of the road.'

'Why did she move to Tudlinghall?'

'Family there already, sir, daughter and grandchildren.'

'Did she see anyone else on the field?' Branton asked.

'She said there was another woman walking a dog, but the fog was so thick that it was hard to see very far ahead, and she couldn't say if there was anyone else there as well.'

'Right. What happened next?'

Mike took up the account. 'Emergency services attended; police team from the city, ambulance with paramedic, two fire engines. There was considerable delay in getting to the deceased as it was unsafe to enter the ditch due to the tractor being at a precarious angle, and sides of ditch steep and very slippery. Paramedic unable to access body to check for vital signs for same reason. Field too muddy for Fire Engine. Garage owner next door to social club was approached and offered a tow-truck to pull the tractor out of the ditch. Attempt to do so failed.'

'Garage owner's name?'

'Peter Morris, sir. 'Minor' to his mates.'

'And are we now his mates?'

'Very much so, sir!'

'Well, at least someone likes us,' Branton said wearily, 'Did he have any other information?'

'Initial identification of the body from our mate Minor. Told emergency attendees that it was likely to be Mr Trevor Fish, caretaker of the Social Club and the adjoining Memorial Hall.'

'Because, presumably, he knew the deceased?'

'Yes, sir. Deceased spent a lot of time on the tractor, so it was probable that it was him. Another woman arrived on the scene, a Ms Mandy Pope, who worked behind the bar at the Social Club. She'd just arrived for work, and was wondering why there was all the emergency services there. She confirmed Mr Fish was not at his usual place of work behind the bar, and became distressed, assuming the body in the ditch was Mr Fish.'

'After an initial statement was taken, Paramedic took charge of Ms Pope, and she was sent home,' Jan went on. 'We got the tractor out of the ditch. Body confirmed as Mr Fish by contents of wallet, and death confirmed by paramedic.'

'How did you get the tractor out of the ditch?'

'Oh, sorry sir, Mr Morris came back with a V8 Landy automatic, and it came out easily.'

'Right. Any other witness statements?'

'Yes, sir, lots, but they're all deaf and blind; no-one heard nothing, no-one saw nothing,' Mike said bitterly. 'Except one.'

'Yes?'

'Guess who the other woman was that Mrs Cooper saw on the playing field that morning?'

'No!' Branton gave a theatrical groan and clutched his head with both hands.

Mike laughed, 'I know, sir, it would have to be her, wouldn't it?'

'Who?' Jan asked, looking from one to the other.

'An interfering old bat called Miss Walsh who lives in Tudlinghall and thinks she knows all about detecting because she was in the police force around the time of the Ark. Watch out for her, she'll pump you for intel and then poke her nose in.' Branton said with some venom.

'Oh, ok,' Jan said with some bafflement, wondering where this sudden vindictiveness had come from.

'She got one right over us on the Coe case,' Branton went on, 'Bit before your time, I think. Mike can fill you in later.'

'Do you mean she solved it?' Jan asked.

'Well, that's what everyone said, but I'm sure we'd have caught the killer far sooner if she hadn't been nosying around and muddying the waters. Anyway, watch out for her.'

'Do you know what she looks like?' Jan asked Mike.

'I haven't met her. Evans took her statement,' Mike said.

'Standard issue old spinster who lives in a village and pokes her nose in wherever it's not wanted,' Branton said shortly.

'If she's a local, she might have some valuable information about the deceased, sir,' Jan pointed out.

'True. Well, if you see her, which I'm sure you will, then get what you can out of her, but don't give her anything back.'

'I'll do my best, sir,' Jan said.

'So, what did our Miss Walsh have to say in her statement?' Branton asked in a world-weary tone.

'She said she heard a diesel engine running, but can't say when it stopped. She saw one other woman on the field, who was walking a Golden Retriever called 'Bella', which was actually male.'

'That, presumably was Mrs Cooper. Anything else?'

'No, that's pretty much it,' Mike said, scanning down Miss Walsh's statement quickly.

'Did she know deceased?'

'Yes, she runs lots of clubs and hires the Memorial Hall regularly, which brought her into contact with him.'

'Of course she does!' Branton said resignedly. 'And according to everyone we've spoken to, including her; deceased was a pillar of the local community, no enemies, loved by all, no doubt?'

'That's about it, sir, except Miss Walsh, who said he was a cantankerous old sod who made life as difficult as possible for everyone who booked the hall.'

'Tell me that didn't go to the Coroner?' Branton asked.

'No sir, it was just in Evans's notes.'

'Good. Well, we've got the press as usual to contend with and we don't want this to be our Una Crown,'* Branton said. 'But apart from Miss Walsh, no-one else said anything that might indicate anyone might want to murder the deceased?'

Jan and Mike shook their heads.

'People do get murdered for being pains in the arse,' Branton went on thoughtfully, 'But let's hope that's not the case here. The post-mortem showed contusion to deceased's back of head, and pathologist speculated he could have been hit on the back of the head either before or after the tractor went into the ditch.'

'So, unless he hit himself over the back of the head, and then somehow got the tractor to roll over to the ditch, someone bashed him somehow while he was on the tractor, and he lost control and veered it into the ditch?' Mike said, 'Which might make it murder after all.'

'Other injuries picked up by the post-mortem are what would be consistent with having a tractor land on him,' Branton went on, reading from the report. 'Back, legs, neck and arms broken, major internal organ ruptures, etc. Oh, and just to make sure he really was dead, there was four inches of water in the ditch, and he landed face down. Post-mortem showed water in his lungs, so he took at least one breath after he landed in the ditch.'

'Was the post-mortem certain that the blow to the back of the head was not caused by the tractor landing on him?' Mike asked.

'No,' Branton said, handing the report to Mike, 'It's listed as a possibility.'

As Jan and Mike skimmed through the summary of findings, Branton went on, 'Right, so it's still unexplained, but possibly murder by person or persons unknown at this stage. Coroner wants an inquest, so we'll need to do more investigation.'

'Yes, sir'.

'Anything else turn up at the site?'

Jan picked up a list; 'A finger-tip search was carried out starting with the area directly beneath the body and the tractor, and widening out to encompass the length of the ditch. In the ditch within two metres of the body was several broken bits of brick, but no blood or tissue residue was found on any surface. Four foam dog balls, two deflated footballs, one used condom, ten empty drinks cans, four empty water bottles, six empty crisp packets, two black bags of dog poop, and ten empty baggies previously containing dope as confirmed by PD Bullet.'

'The rest of the field also had considerable littering, with chip papers, McDonald's bags, disposable coffee cups, nappies, tissues, and till receipts as well as similar items to those found in the ditch,' added Mike.

'Typical playing field haul, then?' grunted DS Branton.

'Yes sir, but nothing had any blood or tissue on from the deceased.'

DS Branton looked again at the post-mortem report. 'Back of skull was fractured, but skin not broken, so it's unlikely there would be blood or tissue on any weapon. Question is, how did someone hit him hard enough to break his skull if he was sitting on his tractor? And if he wasn't on the tractor when they hit him, did they drag him to the ditch, and how did they get the tractor to fall on him without getting injured themselves?'

'Prior to the tractor being removed, we thoroughly examined the area immediately around the site. There was no sign of deceased having been dragged, sir,' Mike said. 'There were no drag marks on the grass leading to the ditch, just tractor tyre marks, and no muddy marks on his shoes or overalls consistent with having been dragged across a damp field.'

'Footprints?'

'Rather a lot, sir,' Jan said ruefully. 'Mrs Cooper, of course approached to see what had happened to the tractor, and her dog ran all over the area as well. There were other older footprints from dog walkers, and horse hoof prints, and deer tracks and fox prints and bird prints. The field sees a lot of activity, and it's been very wet recently, so it was muddy and churned up. It wasn't possible to see if anyone had been walking directly alongside the tractor as it veered towards the ditch.'

'We're probably looking at an accident, but we'll suppose for the moment that somehow someone hit him over the back of the head, perhaps with a long branch, did you see any nearby? And he lost control of the tractor and got flipped into the ditch.'

'There's a woodland on that side of the field, sir, so a branch could have been thrown over there after being used as a weapon.'

'Right, take the dog, get back over to Tudlinghall, find out who owns that woodland, ask their permission to search near the ditch site to see if there's any branches that might have been used. Also look for any other long heavy objects like cricket bats, golf clubs, broom handles, anything that someone could have used to come up behind him and hit him while he was seated on the tractor.'

'Yes, sir.'

'Oh, and there's a memorial service Tuesday 11am, Tudlinghall Church, get-together afterwards at the Social Club. I want you both to attend, mingle with the attendees, take statement forms just in case the service prompts any sudden memories or attacks of conscience. And Jan, get a statement ready for the press; the usual following up all leads, any other information welcome, arrests imminent, that sort of thing.'

'What can I say about the manner of his death?'

'Well, the post-mortem will have been reported in the papers, so if you're asked say currently death is unexplained, but we're not ruling anything out. Now, did deceased have any family, significant others, kids?'

'No sir, he lived alone. But I believe there's a sister living in Tudlinghall.'

'Have we got a statement from her?'

'Yes, sir. She was on the night shift at the hospital, didn't come off duty till 8am, and then had breakfast with colleagues in the canteen before driving home and going straight to bed.'

'Any ex-partners?'

'There was a wife once according to Mr Morris, but they're long estranged, and she lives out at Larmouth.'

'Ask someone at Larmouth to go and see her, offer condolences, see if she can shed any light on it.'

'Yes, sir.'

'Anything else for now?'

Jan and Mike shook their heads, and were dismissed to carry out the various tasks.

*Una Crown was an 86 year old widow who was murdered in her own bungalow. The police badly bungled the subsequent investigation, and the case has not been solved.

Jan and Mike collected PD Bullet and walked up the side of the station towards their patrol car; Bullet was wildly excited about going out.

'Have you got his reward ball?' Jan asked.

'Damn, I'll just go back and get it.' Mike headed back towards the kennels, and Jan put Bullet through some commands to calm him down and focus him on the job ahead. Then she got him to jump up into the cage in the back of the car and checked through the equipment including his tracking harness.

Mike returned with Bullet's reward ball, and Jan asked Mike to tell her about the Coe case as they set off for Tudlinghall.

'I don't remember much, I was a recruit at the time,' Mike said, 'I gather it was similar to the Crown case out at Wisbech, but the Coe one was in Trotwood. Old lady found dead at property, battered to death, and set on fire to try and conceal the evidence.'

'And this Miss Walsh found out who'd done it?'

'Yes, she did.'

'How?' Jan asked as they navigated the frequent speed bumps through Tudlinghall, and inched around all the cars parked along the road near the school.

'No idea, but she let us take all the credit, which really got up the Chief's nose. He passed the grief downwards, and I think Branton may have caught some of it. In my experience, old ladies know a lot more than we give them credit for. I wouldn't write this Miss Walsh off whatever Branton says. It might be worth you cosying up to her, if she turns up.'

'I'll do my best,' Jan said, 'Oh, right here through that gate-way.'

They had arrived.

The property next to the Social Club on the left as you're looking at it, is Tudlinghall Grange. Built in the late 1600s to the early 1700s, and mentioned in the diaries of a bon viveur who lived nearby in the eighteenth century, when it was a Rectory. It was also once the home of a friend of William Cowper, the eighteenth-century poet from the nearby market town. The house sits well back from the road and can't be seen from the road due to the number of trees, which stretch right across the frontage. The trees also screen the house from being seen from the playing field behind the Social Club.

The gates were open and the police car drove up the drive-way opening up out of the trees to lawns on either side of the drive way, with the house crouched at the end.

'It's not as big as I thought it would be,' Jan remarked.

'Probably goes back a long way,' Mike answered, and they got out of the car, Jan put her hat on, and both straightened their jackets.

'Where's the front door?'

The driveway swept round in a circle to go back out again, and the face of the house directly ahead of them had windows but no doors.

'You go left and I'll go right,' Mike said, and they set off. He called almost immediately, and she joined him around the right-hand corner of the building, where there was a large door set in a gothic-looking arched doorway.

'Well, that is impressive,' Jan said quietly, as Mike reached up to the very modern doorbell and pressed it.

A woman opened the door and looked shocked at the sight of two police officers. Accustomed to this reaction, Jan hastily said, 'We're here on routine enquiries, ma'am, after a man was found dead on the playing field which borders this property.'

'Oh dear, I'm sorry to hear that. What happened?'

'Enquiries are on-going, ma'am,' Mike said stolidly.

'I see. Well, would you like to come in?'

Her voice was quite harsh with a distinctly estuary English accent, she was casually dressed, and probably in her late thirties, Jan thought. Jan removed her hat as they followed the woman in to a tiled hall with a carved staircase rising out of it towards a balcony leading to the first floor, and doorways ahead and off to the left and right. She took them left into a brightly upholstered room with book-shelves on the side walls, and very large windows cut almost to the ground facing the door. These were the windows they had seen when they arrived, and their car was visible on the driveway outside. The sofas were very low and the two police officers lowered themselves very cautiously down.

'How can I help you?' the woman asked.

Jan took out her notepad and pencil, ready to make notes, but a glance at Mike saw that he had done the same, and was waiting for her to speak to the woman.

'If we could take your name, please?' Jan asked.

'I'm Liz, Elizabeth Harte, I mean.'

'And do you live here alone?'

'Oh no, this is my dad's house, he built an annexe on for me.'

'And is your dad at home?'

'No, he's away at present, for work.'

'So, you're looking after the house for him?'

'Yes, I suppose you could say that. Oh! I've just had a thought!'

'What's that?' Jan asked.

'Well, I host a book group in this room once a week, and they're all due in half an hour's time. They come in here because I don't have a room big enough for them all in my annexe.'

Jan looked at Mike asking silently if they really wanted a load of people turning up in half an hour's time while they were searching the grounds?

Mike took the hint. 'Ms Harte, we would like to ask your permission to search the woodland of your property which borders the playing field, and we might be hampered in that investigation if lots of other people come on to the property at the same time. Is it possible for you to cancel your book group?'

'Or arrange for them to meet up at someone else's house?' Jan put in.

Liz Harte looked flustered, 'Well, of course you can search the grounds, but I don't know what you expect to find?'

'It's just a matter of routine, Ms Harte,' Mike said soothingly, 'We will also be searching Mr Morris's grounds and the grounds of number 41 which also runs alongside the sports field on the other side.'

'I see, well, let me make some phone calls and I'll see if I can divert the book group to another member's house just up the road.'

'That would be very helpful, thank you, Ms Harte,' Mike said, and both officers stood up as the woman left the room.

They could hear her voice coming from the hall, and Jan moved silently to the doorway to overhear Mrs Harte's half of the conversation at least.

'Hello, it's me.'

'I'm going to have to cancel this morning, I'm afraid, the police have arrived.'

'No, it's about that man who died.'

'Yes, so you can't come here.'

'I think that would be best.'

'Thanks. Let me know how it goes.'

'Great, thanks, bye.'

Jan returned silently to her sofa as Ms Harte came back into the room.

'That's all right, Anna up the road will host, and she's going to ring around everyone for me. Now, do you need me to be here while you are searching?'

'It would be helpful if you could remain on the property, in case we find anything that you may be able to identify as belonging to your family, and therefore not part of the investigation,' Jan said.

'I see, very well,' Ms Harte said, 'Now can I offer you anything before you start? A cup of coffee? I bought biscuits for the meeting, and I can't eat them all on my own.'

The two officers followed Liz Harte back into the hall, and she turned sharp left down quite a narrow dark corridor which passed underneath the gallery landing, and past a smaller staircase on the right, then a dining room, and finally came out into a modern kitchen with floor to ceiling doors looking out on to a terrace and lawns.

'Does anyone else live in the annexe with you, Ms Harte?' asked Jan, as they all sat down at a large kitchen island with their coffee, and a plate of biscuits.

'No, I'm divorced, and I live there on my own. My parents live in the main house, as I said.'

'And they're both away at the moment?'

'Yes, they have a house in Portugal, and business interests there. So they go between the two houses.'

'When did they leave?' Mike asked, hoping to eliminate them from the enquiries.

'Two months ago, and they'll be back next week.'

'Thank you.'

They ate and drank in silence for a while, and then Jan said, 'Well, we'd better get the dog out of the car, and start the search.'

'Oh, do you have a police dog with you?' Liz Harte said, 'I love dogs, as you can see.'

There were two slumbering dogs in baskets in a corner of the kitchen, which had sleepily raised their heads and wagged their tails when they saw the humans enter, and then returned to their interrupted nap.

'If you would keep the dogs indoors until we leave, that would be very helpful,' Mike said.

'These two are not going anywhere,' Liz Harte said fondly, 'They're much too lazy; it's all I can do to get them out for a walk around the garden once a day when my parents are away. Dad takes them for long walks when he's home.'

The dogs' ears pricked up a bit at the word 'walk', but drooped again when it was clear no-one was expecting them to get up.

Liz Harte added, 'It's nice to have dogs, although the mum's getting old now, and the younger one is much too lazy to be a fierce watch-dog. Anyway, Tudlinghall is such a peaceful safe place, well, apart from that poor man, but I suppose it was an accident?'

'That's what we are hoping to establish,' Jan said, as both officers stood up.

'Now to get out again, you can either go back out through the front door, or out this door around the house to either side, it'll bring you back to the drive.'

'We'll follow you back to the front door,' Jan said, and they trooped in procession back through the hall and out into the driveway again. Jan let Bullet out of the car and he ran two circuits of the lawned area at top speed before she called him to have his harness put on, and he came straight to her and sat down while she adjusted the harness.

'He's very well trained,' Liz Harte said, 'My dogs are hopeless at recall.'

Bullet was now soberly trotting at Jan's side, and Mike said, 'We'll come back and let you know when we've finished, and if we find anything.'

Liz Harte watched as the two officers got their bearings and headed off into the woods towards the boundary with the sports field, the dog already beginning to quest with its nose through the undergrowth.

CHAPTER EIGHT: A BIT OF MORTUIIS NIL NISI BONUM

The search of Tudlinghall Grange woods didn't turn-up anything that could reasonably have been used to hit Trevor Fish over the back of the head and then be thrown over a fence. There certainly were branches aplenty, but PD Bullet wasn't interested in any of them, and his two handlers had long learned to trust to his judgement on such matters.

They gave him his reward ball when they returned to the car, and called briefly on Ms Harte to tell her that they hadn't found anything of concern in her grounds. Then they called on Mr Morris, and the owners of number 41, but their gardens were far less wild than the woods at Tudlinghall Grange, and it was soon clear that there was nothing of interest in either of them.

They were back at their Police Station updating DS Branton in time for a late lunch.

'Well done,' he said, 'One last push at the memorial service, and then we'll pass all our reports on to the Coroner, and I expect the verdict will be accidental death on balance of probabilities.'

A secretary put her head round the door and said, 'Report in from a garage in Tudlinghall.'

Jan took it and scanned through it, 'Mr Morris says the tractor belonging to the deceased hadn't been properly maintained, but that there was nothing wrong with the brakes. It might have failed to start if the deceased had continued not maintaining it, but it wouldn't have failed to brake.'

She passed it to Mike, who also scanned through it before handing to DS Branton.

'The last piece is the surgery in Tudlinghall should be sending us a report on the victim's health, sir,' Jan said, 'It may be that he had heart problems, or high risk of stroke or something which might explain him losing consciousness on the tractor.'

'Hopefully that'll be with us by the time you go to the memorial service, then we can wrap it all up,' Branton said, but the surgery was clearly too busy and the report didn't arrive before the Tuesday.

While the Police had been diligently searching the Playing field and the properties to either side of the Memorial Hall grounds, Miss Walsh had equally diligently been walking Truncheon past the still taped-off gates. To her extreme annoyance, none of the police officers on duty were familiar to her, and none were inclined to talk, or even make a fuss of Trunch, who was at his most fluffy and appealing after a visit to the dog groomer. Usually even the hardest police heart was softened by the sight of a former Police Dog, but not on this occasion. Miss Walsh was not to know that Inspector Branton's disapproval of interfering amateurs had percolated right down to the lowliest coppers on duty, and that they were following his implicit instructions not to talk to anyone about the case.

Instead, she decided to wait until after the Memorial service before launching an investigation proper of her own. By then, the police presence at the Social Club would be stood down, as it was doubtful they would find anything else of any significance at the site after nearly four weeks had passed since the body was found. For now, Miss Walsh decided to focus on the service in Trevor's memory, and so she and Marjorie had spent a happy morning conferring on what they should wear to the Memorial Service. Neither was in mourning for Trevor, but both wanted to be respectful; after all, the poor man was dead before his time. They decided on dark colours; a navy-blue skirt and jacket for Marjorie, underneath her navy winter coat, and dark brown for Miss Walsh under her serviceable camel trench coat.

Knowing that Church Plain would be packed with cars left by carefree shoppers as well as those actually attending who were too lazy or infirm to walk, the two women walked down Mill Street towards the Church. There were indeed a lot of cars already there, and as they arrived, a police car also arrived and squeezed in to a space.

Miss Walsh watched as two officers, one in uniform, one plain clothes, got out of the car. She didn't recognise either of them from her past dealings with the local town's police station, but hoped that the woman officer at least might be friendly. Marjorie nudged her and nodded ostentatiously at the two officers.

'Yes, I see them,' Miss Walsh said sotto voce, 'I'll see what I can find out if they come to the Memorial Hall afterwards.'

Mike noticed they were being observed by two soberly dressed older women and indicated with a flick of his eye-brows to Jan. 'Think one of them's her?' Jan asked under her breath.

'Highly likely,' Mike replied, equally quietly, as they made their way up the paved path to the church porch.

'Which one? Blue or brown?'

'I'd put a fiver on blue,' Mike said.

'Ok, I'll bet brown.'

***

The memorial service for Trevor Fish, late caretaker, and bachelor of the parish of Tudlinghall, was held at All Saints Church, followed by refreshments at the Social Club.

The attendance was surprisingly large given that Trevor had managed to piss off just about everyone in the village at some point or other, but could probably be explained by curiosity, and the chance of some free nosh and a cup of tea or coffee afterwards. No-one had quite enough cheek to just turn up to the gathering without going to the service first. Mandy Pope didn't attend the service as she was busy making all the arrangements for setting out the refreshments, provided by Dodgers on Church Plain, and paid for by the charity which ran the Social Club.

Jan and Mike sat at the back of the church and spent the service observing the congregation. The vicar did her best with scant material; but with a good deal more de mortuis than many people there probably felt. Although the Vicar hadn't ever needed to book the Memorial Hall as there was a well-equipped Church Hall across the road from the Church, she was well aware of Trevor's reputation in the village as a cantankerous and unhelpful custodian. Despite that, as Miss Walsh had pointed out to

Marjorie, the poor man had died in strange circumstances, and so the Vicar felt able to say,

'Trevor Fish was a well-known person in the village, a dedicated caretaker of the Social Club, and his sudden death has been a shock to us all. We are gathered here today to pray for him, and to thank God for his life ...'

There was a woman in her late middle age being treated very solicitously by the vicar, and sitting right at the front of the church in a pew where family would normally sit for big events like weddings, christenings, and funerals. Out of some sort of unspoken deference, no-one else was sitting in the two front pews on either side of the Church. The woman left isolated by this deference was dressed in black from head to foot, and although she hadn't gone quite as far as wearing a veil, she clearly intended everyone to know she was in the deepest mourning possible. Mike gave Jan a tiny nod, and Jan knew he meant that woman was clearly someone to cultivate at the after-service get-together.

All heads swivelled round to look at the representatives of the Law at the back of the church when the vicar reminded the congregation that Trevor's body had not yet been released for burial, and that enquiries into his sudden death were on-going.

After that, the service was mercifully short; and Jan wondered who would organise the funeral in the absence of any known family; possibly the woman in black? Was she Trevor's new love, or his ex-wife? Jan hoped he'd made a Will stating who would organise the funeral and where any money went – Wills were always a good motive for a murder, and eliminating that motive might help steer the Coroner's mind towards Death by Misadventure. She jotted a quick note to remind herself to check up on that, just as the congregation all stood and began leaving the Church in subdued clusters. The woman all in black was pressing a handkerchief to her eyes as she was escorted out by the Vicar; Jan and Mike stood and waited respectfully until everyone else had filed out past them, including the women in brown and blue they had noticed earlier.

'Should we wait here and try and talk to the police?' Marjorie asked as they exited the Church porch, but Miss Walsh shook her head.

'No, I'll wait till we get to the Memorial Hall,' she said, and they set off as fast as they could in that direction.

Church Plain emptied of cars as everyone headed up Church Street towards West Green and the Social Club, where Trevor had met his unfortunate end. Jan and Mike sat in their Panda car and watched them all pull away.

'Who on earth has a black-bordered handkerchief these days?' Jan marvelled.

'A grieving widow should always have a proper handkerchief,' Mike said sonorously.

'Do you think she was a grieving widow?' Jan asked.

'You get her talking, we might be able to find out.'

'All right then, and I haven't forgotten our bet over Miss Walsh either,' Jan said, as she steered the car cautiously out on to Church Street.

CHAPTER NINE: THE POLICE MINGLE

The party seemed to be already quite lively by the time the police officers joined the mourners even though there wasn't any music. An enormous flat screen television showing a football match was providing vision but not sound on one wall. The sound was all coming from people who, like people tend to do, had become voluble when relieved that a sombre occasion is over. There was a large table along one wall covered in plates of food, and two women were standing by a steaming urn dispensing tea and coffee. In deference to the fact that it was the middle of a working day, and most people had driven there, the bar was not available, but a notice informed those present that the bar would be open in Trevor's honour later that evening, and the first drink would be on the house.

'Right,' said Mike, looking around as they entered the room, 'Mingle.'

Their arrival was greeted with the usual slightly disconcerting silence which greets the appearance of anyone on the side of law and order, who are separated from the rest of humanity by an assumed inhuman quantity of law-abiding virtue, and their societally sanctioned ability to arrest and detain.

Jan headed across the room towards the apparent widow, and Mike made his way to the buffet. Years of experience had taught him that women of a certain age love to press food on younger men, and that hovering over the buffet and looking hungry was a good way to get said women talking. He didn't have to pretend too hard to be hungry as breakfast had been some time ago, and it was now quite late for lunch anyway. He soon had the two women laughing bashfully, and insisting he tried this cake and that scone, and it was then easy to engage them in conversation about the reason for this party.

'Oh that Trevor,' one of the women said, 'He were a right rum un, he were.'

'What are you like?' the other woman said, 'You mustn't speak ill of the dead.'

'Whyever not?' the first woman countered, 'They can't do nothing about it, he can't hear me and even if he could, he knew what I thought about him.'

'Why are you even here then?' the first woman said, rather crossly.

The second woman gestured at the spread before them, and added, 'And I'm Mandy's friend, I'm here for her.'

'Is she very upset by Trevor's death?' Mike put in adroitly.

'Oh yes, she were ever so upset,' the second woman said, 'They worked together for years and he didn't mess her about like he did some people.'

'Were they … ?' Mike enquired delicately; certain the two women would understand what he was insinuating.

'Oh no, nothing like that!' the first woman said, 'He were a lot older than her, and anyway … '

What she was going to say was lost as another punter came forward to investigate the refreshments, and both women sprang into competitive action with the tea-cups and urn, and welcoming smiles for the newcomer.

Mike moved to a nearby table, which was occupied by four people, and pulled up a chair indicating he wanted to sit with them; they obligingly moved aside, and he put his very full plate down on the table.

Conversation at that table immediately died, and all faces turned to look expectantly at him. One of them was Mandy, and Mike hoped she'd recognise him and give him an entrée to the other guests.

'This is the policeman what's investigating Trevor's death,' Mandy said, and everyone nodded solemnly.

'How are you doing, Mandy?' Mike asked, doing his best to look winsome and unthreatening. Tucking into a sandwich definitely helped.

'Up and down,' Mandy said with a sigh, 'I miss the old bugger.'

'I'm sure you do,' Mike said soothingly, but was unable to extract any more information from her as she was called away by one of the ladies on the buffet with some question about extra cups.

'She'll not have long to miss him,' one of the other people at the table confided.

'Oh? Why's that?' Mike asked, starting on another sandwich.

'There's got to be a caretaker,' the person said, 'And she don't want the job, so they'll have to advertise.'

'They won't put an advert in till he's been decently buried,' said another slightly reprovingly.

'No, they won't,' the first person said, 'That wouldn't be respectful, she say.'

'Mandy?' Trevor asked, and they all nodded. 'How does she feel about working with someone new?'

'That won't be someone new,' the first person said knowingly, 'She already know him.'

'But they still got to advertise, to make it fair,' the second person said. 'But he'll get the job, no doubt about it.'

'Who will?' Mike asked, somewhat indistinctly through a large mouthful of cake. He took a hasty swallow of the lukewarm tea, and tipped his head to one side as though to hear better.

'Ol' Malcolm Savoury over there,' the first person said. 'He's been in line for the job for years.'

'But Trevor weren't giving it up any time soon,' the first person said, 'He said he didn't want to retire, and he needed the money anyway.'

Mike looked around at the man indicated, who was sitting peaceably at a table nearby with several other people, drinking tea, and eating a fairy cake. If these people were to be believed, here was a possible motive for murder, but mindful of how long they had spent at the event already, Mike decided not to probe for any more information, but move on to another group to see if they had any other helpful information. He had the name of Trevor's rival for the caretaker role, and it was doubtful that Mr Savoury would flee the country any time soon.

It was time to ascertain which of the two women they'd seen outside the church was the redoubtable Miss, formerly Inspector, Walsh. Accordingly, he threaded his way through the crowd to a small group of women comprising the two in blue and brown, and they both turned obligingly towards him as he approached.

While Mike had been charming the ladies on the buffet and tracking down Miss Walsh, Jan had taken her time to walk across the room towards the woman in black; it was part of her training to assess situations before engaging with anyone. The room seemed to have split into two camps, with a woman at the centre of each. In one area was a small group of older women, gathered around the woman in black. They appeared to be sympathetic towards her, and were nodding and giving her little pats on the arm or the hand as she talked and wielded her handkerchief.

Far more people were either sitting at the tables with plates and cups, or gathered around another middle-aged woman who was far less elaborately dressed, but still managed to convey grief in her choice of clothing. As Jan watched, one woman detached from the group around the woman in black, made a less than convincing detour via the buffet, and then joined the other group, but in a position which was not visible to the woman in black. As Jan watched, the other women also appeared to make excuses to walk away towards the buffet or the tables, and so the field was clear for her to approach the woman herself.

As may have seemed obvious, she was Trevor's widow; what was less obvious was that they had been estranged for decades, and that their parting had been so acrimonious that neither had wanted to set eyes on the other until they were safely in their coffin. It seemed that Tish, at least, had achieved that wish.

'Tish?' Jan asked, after the introductions had been made.

'Short for Patricia,' Tish said, 'But everyone calls me 'Tish'.'

'Well, Tish, may I ask you a few questions?'

'Of course,' Tish said, adopting that wide-eyed look of absolute innocence which people hope will persuade police officers that they have nothing to hide, but which immediately makes them appear much more suspicious. 'But I already talked to the policeman what come out to see me and tell me about Trevor.'

Jan ignored this attempt to dodge any further questions, and asked, 'You live in Larmouth?'

'Yes, I do now, but I used to live here with Trevor.' She gestured around vaguely, but Jan doubted they'd lived at the Social Club, and decided she probably meant in Tudlinghall somewhere.

'How long have you lived in Larmouth for?'

'Oh, not that long, might be five years?' Tish was clearly lying; her gaze was no longer steady or wide-eyed, but rather furtive and twitchy.

'And did Trevor join you at Larmouth when he was able to get away from work?'

'No,' Tish said rather unwillingly. Then, as she couldn't see any way of avoiding the inevitable question, she added, 'We was taking a break.'

'A break?'

'From each other, if you see what I mean?'

'You were separated?' Jan asked.

'Not formally, not properly, we weren't divorced or nothing, just spending a bit of time apart, to think about our options, if you like.'

'Do you think you might have got back together?' Jan asked.

Tish gave a sob, which sounded very theatrical to Jan, and out came the handkerchief again, but Jan could see there were no tears, and that Tish was very careful to press the handkerchief where it wouldn't disturb her make-up.

'Would you excuse me a moment?' Tish asked in a tiny voice, and moved away before Jan could say yes or no.

'She's a lying old trout,' a woman's voice came from behind Jan, and she turned around to see the other middle-aged woman who had moved away from her supporters and may have been the reason that Tish had left so precipitately.

'They han't lived together for thirty year. I'm Sandra, Trevor's sister,' the woman said.

'I'm very pleased to meet you,' Jan said.

'Are you investigating his murder?' Sandra asked bluntly.

'Do you think he was murdered?' Jan countered.

'Of course he were, and I know who by as well.'

Jan looked all interested enquiry, and Sandra was emboldened to continue. She beckoned Jan to lean forward and whispered loudly, 'By that old trout, that's who by, and I told that other policeman what took my statement so and all.'

'Why would you think she murdered him?' Jan asked.

'She's a grasping old cow that one. Took Trevor for every penny while they was together, and tried to screw the last few out of him when she left him, but he weren't having it.'

'What do you mean?'

'He wouldn't sign them divorce papers what she sent him, cos he didn't agree she should have the house and everything when she were the one what left him.'

'I see,' Jan said, 'So you think … ?' Like Mike, she had learned that starting a sentence encouraged people to fill in the rest themselves.

'Yes, she murdered him all right, and she's hoping he han't changed his Will so she'll get the lot after all.'

This certainly raised some interesting questions, but all Jan said was, 'Did Trevor leave a lot of money?'

'We'll find out soon enough,' Sandra said, 'She's got an appointment to see a solicitor after this.'

Jan remembered the woman who had moved circuitously from Tish's group to Sandra's and wondered if she'd passed that information on, but before she could investigate Sandra's suspicions about Tish any further, Sandra said, 'Oh she's off, I'd best be going too,' and darted away.

Jan looked round to see the rather lonely figure of Tish heading out of the door. Mike had also noticed, and made his apologies to Miss Walsh and Marjorie, and met Jan at the doorway. As they left the room together they were aware of the sudden rise in volume of enjoyment and conversation at their departure.

CHAPTER TEN: WILLS, WIVES AND WRECKS

In the car, as they drove at a discreet distance behind Tish's car, Jan and Mike brought each other up to date with everything they'd learned at the party, which took them most of the way back to the market town.

But first, Mike handed Jan a fiver. 'Brown, then?' she said, tucking it away in a pocket.

'Yep, brown,' Mike replied. 'I've said you'll call round to see her, and were keen to hear what she had to say.'

'Oh, thank you,' Jan said.

'It's what the Chief would want,' Mike said solemnly, which made Jan laugh.

'What else did you find out?' she asked.

'Well, we've got two possible motives for murder,' Mike said thoughtfully, 'The widow, and the guy who wanted his job.'

'Do you really think he was murdered by one of them?'

'No, but it would be one of them if it were a detective story, that's for sure.'

'Which solicitor do you think she's going to?' Jan asked.

'Want to lay a bet?' Mike asked, 'I'll win that fiver back off you by saying, Good, Moore and Hallwood.'

'Ok,' Jan said, 'I'll go for … Mann, Smythe and Butcher, then.'

They both lost the bet as Tish parked across two spaces on Church Street, and tottered up to the door of Tower Solicitors, where Sandra was waiting for her having broken every speed limit in her determination to arrive first.

'Aye, aye,' said Mike, 'Trouble at Mill.'

They pulled in behind Tish's car and both got out of the car as fast as they could as the two women launched themselves at each other, screaming and raining blows on each other.

Jan and Mike ran towards them, and pulled them apart. Mike drew the short straw and got Tish all limp and weeping in his arms, while Jan had quite a job restraining Sandra, and was just considering hand-cuffs when she suddenly subsided.

'What's all this about, then?' Mike asked.

'She's no right to his money, she in't his wife no more!' was Sandra's contribution to clarity.

'I am his wife,' Tish sobbed. Jan noted with interest that there were real tears now, and that her carefully applied makeup was running down her face.

'You are not! You left him, you don't deserve nothing!' Sandra retorted.

'I'm still his wife!'

'You're not!'

'He never signed no papers!'

'You left him!'

Before things got any more childish, Jan intervened, 'Do you have an appointment to see a solicitor now, Mrs Fish?'

Sandra snorted at the 'Mrs Fish', but Tish replied, 'Yes, at three. But she's not allowed in. She's not in his Will.'

'How do you know? He might-a changed it after you left him!' Sandra shouted back defiantly.

'She can't come in, can she?' Tish said in a wobbly voice, looking up wide-eyed at Mike, hoping for support.

'Just try and stop me!' Sandra shouted back again.

'May I be of any help, officers?' another voice cut in, and everyone turned to look at a tall rangy looking woman in her late middle-age, soberly dressed in a camel-coloured trench coat, and wearing a dark brown hat. 'I was just doing a bit of shopping,' Miss Walsh said, holding up two carrier bags as evidence (no-one needed to know that they contained a pair of wellington boots and a raincoat that she always kept in the boot of the car), 'and I noticed that there was a bit of an altercation.'

When no-one answered, she said to Mike, 'We met earlier at the Memorial Hall.' And to Sandra and Tish, she added, I'm retired Police Inspector Leonie Walsh.'

They both said, 'Hello,' in small voices, wondering what was going to happen next. Miss Walsh now had everyone's attention. Despite being retired, she had once out-ranked Jan and Mike, and they were also waiting to see what she would do next.

She addressed herself to the two serving police officers. 'Now, I'm sure you have much more pressing matters to attend to officers, and so I'm happy to escort these two ladies in to see the solicitor, if it would help?'

Jan had to admire the way that Miss Walsh had seamlessly inserted herself into the case, but also had to admit that it wasn't a good use of police time to attend a Will reading, no matter how combative the participants may have been. She caught Mike's eye, and he nodded imperceptibly.

'Thank you, Miss Walsh. We'll just see you in to the office, and then we'll leave you to it.'

Miss Walsh followed the others into the Reception area, and stashed her two carrier bags next to a tall potted plant. The Receptionist looked rather alarmed at the sight of two police officers escorting in two rather dishevelled women, but her training kicked in and she politely asked if she could help them.

'I've got an appointment to see Mr Rogers about my husband's Will,' Tish said more firmly now that she had support.

'He weren't her husband no more,' Sandra said loudly, but Jan shushed her and she subsided again.

'Er .. that's Ms Rogers,' the Receptionist said, 'I'll let her know you're here. Would anyone like a cup of tea or coffee? Or a glass of water?'

Everyone declined except Tish, who asked for a glass of water.

Sandra rolled her eyes, but didn't say anything, and they all followed the Receptionist through a door, up some stairs, along a corridor and into an office. A young woman rose to greet them, managing to look as though the presence of two police officers with the grieving family was quite normal. Everyone introduced themselves, and then Tish said, 'I'm the one what made the appointment because my husband has died.'

'I am sorry for your loss,' Ms Roger said, and Sandra muttered something about it being *her* loss, not Tish's, but no-one replied.

'We'll leave you now,' Mike said, and added, 'Thank you,' to Miss Walsh, who nodded, and the two police officers left.

'If you would all like to take a seat?' Ms Rogers said, and by unspoken consent the two combatants took chairs on either side of Miss Walsh, which made her feel rather like a parent who has to sit in between two unruly children to make sure they behave.

'If everyone is happy to proceed?' Ms Rogers went on, looking at them all in turn. All nodded, although Tish looked distinctly nervous.

Ms Rogers picked up a piece of paper and said briskly, 'Mr Fish made a Will on 10th December 1992, which invalidated any Will he had previously had drawn up.'

'Told you,' Sandra said in a slightly louder voice, peering round Miss Walsh to nod significantly at Tish. 'Just after she left him.'

Ms Rogers waited to see if anyone wanted to say anything in response, but nobody did. Tish was staring wide-eyed at her, clutching a glass of water with one hand, and her rather damp and mascara-streaked handkerchief with the other. When no-one spoke, Ms Rogers continued.

'It was a simple Will witnessed by two staff members here, with one of my colleagues given as the executor. The house and all possessions therein at the time of Mr Fish's death go to Mrs Sandra Richardson, his sister.'

'That's me,' Sandra said.

'And the contents of his Bank Account go to The Ouse Valley Group of the National Vintage Tractor and Engine Club, once all fees and burial payments have been met from that account. The funeral is to be arranged by Mrs Richardson, or in the event of her predeceasing him, by the executor, which is my colleague, Mr McGregor.'

There was a strangled sound from Tish, and then a thud as she slipped to the floor in a dead faint.

'Hah!' Sandra said in great satisfaction, 'That's cooked her goose all right!'

Miss Walsh knelt beside Tish and swiftly moved her into the recovery position.

'Oh dear,' Ms Rogers said, peering over her desk, 'Is she all right? Should I call an ambulance?'

'Don't you worry bout her,' Sandra said cheerfully, 'Tough as old boots she is. Ten to one she's shamming anyway.'

'I am not,' Tish said indignantly, grasping Miss Walsh's hand to pull herself up and sliding back into her chair. 'He left everything to a Tractor society? Why would he leave them his money? What about me? What I am supposed to do now? This is all your fault!' She turned on Sandra. 'You poisoned his mind against me, you got him to change his Will, I want this Will overturned at once!' This to Ms Rogers. 'I'm his wife, he left it all to me! We made our Wills together when we got married, everything to each other, nothing to anyone else! Specially not her!'

Despite all this verbal provocation, Sandra was sitting back in her chair looking like the cat that had got the cream. She said nothing, but just smiled infuriatingly at her former sister-in-law.

'I'm sorry, Mrs Fish,' Ms Rogers said, 'But these are the provisions of the Will Mr Fish drew up, but as his wife you are entitled to challenge the Will and apply for Reasonable Provision for an Estranged Spouse, and I can provide you with assistance to do so, if you wish. Or I have colleagues who also specialise in Wills who will be happy to assist you.'

'But they was estranged!' Sandra burst out in her turn. 'They wasn't living with each other and she kept trying to get him to divorce her!'

'I did not!'

'Yes you did!'

'There is no point in prolonging this conversation,' Miss Walsh said firmly, standing up. 'Thank you for your time, Ms Rogers. Mrs Richardson, if you would accompany me outside, please?'

Sandra stood up rather uncertainly. 'What about me?' she said, 'Can't I talk to someone about this?'

'Of course,' Ms Rogers said, 'Choose a solicitor and make an appointment, and they will advise you.'

'Can't I talk to you?' Sandra asked. Suddenly all her cockiness was gone, and she seemed deflated, and less threatening.

'I don't think that would be appropriate,' Ms Rogers said, 'But I have lots of colleagues, or there are other solicitors in town and in the city for you to choose from.'

'Come along,' Miss Walsh said not unkindly, and the two of them left Tish with Ms Rogers, and trooped back down the stairs. When they reached the reception, Sandra seemed to regain some of her fight, and insisted on booking an appointment for herself.

'And don't you worry,' she said to Miss Walsh, 'I aren't going to start nothing with her again. We'll fight it out in court if we have to, but she's not getting a penny of my brother's money, nor a single stick of furniture from his house if I have anything to do with it.'

'I'll escort you back to your car just to make sure,' Miss Walsh said firmly. Sandra made the appointment for the following day to see a Mr Carrick, and then docilely followed Miss Walsh back to her own car.

'I'm going straight to the house to have a look around,' she said, suddenly looking forlorn. 'I got a set of keys here. He were my brother, you know, the only family I had left.'

'Would you like me to come with you?' Miss Walsh asked.

'Oh, would you?' Sandra said.

'I'll follow on in my car,' Miss Walsh said, and they drove in a little convoy back to the small bungalow Trevor had occupied on Three Keys Way.

Sandra was standing leaning on her car when Miss Walsh pulled up, having been held up at the junction with Back Lane.

'We grew up here,' she said wistfully, 'Me and him, with our parents. It's only right I get the house now. Mum give it him when she died because he lived there with her and took care of her and dad while he was alive, bless him.'

Miss Walsh looked sympathetic.

'I just can't let her have the house,' she said, 'it's not fair.'

Miss Walsh handed her a paper tissue while reflecting that the law had little to do with fairness as understood by ordinary people.

'If they are still legally married, she may be entitled to half of his assets, but she'd probably have to go to court first,' Miss Walsh said.

'Don't his Will mean anything, then?' Sandra said indignantly. 'He left the house to me, why should she have half of it?'

'Your solicitor will advise you,' Miss Walsh said, 'It's not an area I know much about, never having been married myself.'

'Don't blame you,' Sandra said, 'Too bloody complicated.'

Sandra led the way up the short concrete path. Miss Walsh looked at the unkempt wilderness of the tiny front garden on either side of the path. It appeared the late Mr Fish had not been a keen gardener at home, despite his fervent attention to the grass on the playing field. Inside was a narrow hall-way leading straight down to the toilet at the far end; the door had been left open. There were four other doors leading off the hall-way; and as Sandra pushed each one open, Miss Walsh could see that the late Mr Fish had not been keen on housework either. As a police officer at various ranks, she had seen inside the homes of many people; and she had certain expectations of a home occupied by a single man. They tended to feature piles of unwashed clothing, stacked up take-away containers, and un-hoovered carpets: Trevor ticked all the boxes.

'Mum would have a fit if she could see this,' Sandra said, gloomily peering in through the lounge doorway, with Miss Walsh peering over her shoulder. 'This was my parents' room,' she went on, opening the first door on the right. 'That were my room,' pointing to the second door on the right, 'And this were Trevor's room,' as she opened the second door on the left. The bedroom which had belonged to his parents had not been touched since they died, and was tidy, if shabby. While Sandra's childhood bedroom still had her 'Jackie' posters of David Cassidy on the walls, but all the furniture had gone, leaving a rather desolate looking empty space.

The first door on the left had a television and a sofa in it, so Miss Walsh assumed that had always been the family living room. It was also doubling up as a wardrobe and laundry room, as Trevor appeared to have strung a washing line along one wall from which were hanging a number of what Miss Walsh's mother would have called 'Smalls'.

The two women walked on and reached the end of the hall-way, and then peered in to the toilet room. It bore a definite resemblance to the one Miss Walsh remembered seeing in 'Trainspotting.' Sandra didn't say anything, but turned right into a kitchen extension which had probably not been updated since the house was built. Beyond the kitchen was a very small lobby area with a back door, and another door into a bathroom, which was in a similar state to the toilet room.

'Well, this'll take some cleaning up,' Sandra said gloomily.

'You could get a cleaning company in,' Miss Walsh suggested.

'I might do that and all,' Sandra said, 'But I best have a look through all the rooms in case there's anything valuable or personal. I don't want her getting her hands on it. I'll start in the front room, and if I find anything, I'm taking it home with me. She int got an inventory of contents, have she?'

'I'll just have a look out the back, if I may?' Miss Walsh asked.

'Go ahead,' Sandra called as she headed back through the kitchen.

The key was in the lock, and turned easily, the door opened inwards, and Miss Walsh stepped out cautiously. The back garden was small and square, and there was the rusting frame of a swing which had long lost its chains and seat. There were also several sheds in various stages of decrepitude, and the rest of the space was occupied by two vintage tractors which Trevor appeared to have been dismantling; tools and parts lay all around on bits of old sack and plastic bags. Miss Walsh walked around the house to see how Trevor had got them in to the back garden, and there had once been enough room down one side of the house, which had since been filled up with an assortment of items of limited appeal and no apparent use.

There was nothing of interest out there, and so she returned to the house, and found Sandra in the living room.

'I found all his papers,' she said, holding them up to show Miss Walsh, 'I think I'll take them home and have a look through. It's been a hard day, and I'm really tired now.'

'Good idea,' Miss Walsh said, 'Lock it all up well, and it'll be quite safe.'

'I'll come back tomorrow,' Sandra said as they left the house and she locked the front door. 'Thanks for coming with me.'

'You're very welcome,' Miss Walsh said, and drove thoughtfully back up Back Lane to the junction with the main road, where she had to concentrate over the staggered crossing, and past Church Plain, and then she drove slowly past the Memorial Hall, and there were still lots of cars, so the party was still in full swing.

She decided not to go back in, but instead to go back and fill Marjorie in on what had happened since she'd left the party in hot pursuit of the interested parties, and the police.

Marjorie was gratifying impressed by her account, and they went to discuss the latest village scandals including dark suspicions that the youth were taking drugs and breaking in to the school to steal televisions and laptops, before Miss Walsh said she'd better head home in order to take Trunch out for his afternoon walkies.

Meanwhile the Tudlinghall Surgery had finally got their report in to the police about the state of Trevor's health at the time of his death. Malcolm Savoury had a rock-solid alibi for the day of the death; he was working all that week at Diss, and had been setting off for work at 5am each morning, and not returning until after 9pm. Tish had been at work cleaning for a holiday rental company at a resort twenty miles along the coast from her home, and fortunately for her, a trainee had shadowed her all day to learn the job. All reports were passed to the Coroner, and Jan and Mike were moved on to other cases, including another in Tudlinghall – complaints about drug taking on the village green.

CHAPTER TWELVE: THE INQUEST RULES, AND CASE CLOSED

The Inquest into the untimely death of Trevor Fish finally concluded that the death was due to an accident. The Coroner acknowledged that there was a case for Death by Misadventure due to the fact that Trevor had not properly maintained his tractor, and had played fast and loose with his health, however, there was no evidence that he had died as a result of refusing to take medication to deal with high blood pressure and high cholesterol. The injuries he sustained, which led directly to his death, were consistent with a tractor running out of control, tipping him into the ditch and then falling in on top of him. There was suspicion but no evidence that deceased had suffered a heart attack or a stroke leading him to lose control of the tractor on that fateful day, as otherwise he might have attempted to jump off the tractor as it veered out of control.

The Coroner had taken her time to read through all the evidence available, and finally concluded that it was a tragic accident, but did advise anyone working with machinery to ensure it was properly maintained, and for everyone to listen to their GP and take any medication offered which might prevent their untimely demise.

The rather lengthy ruling was reported in full in the *Eastern Daily Press*, and also merited a short follow-up by *Look East*, although it was not thought necessary to dispatch a reporter to the scene this time, as there was no suspicion of murder.

Case closed for the Police; time to get on with attempting to defeat the latest County Lines drug dealers, who had Hydra-like sprung back into being, despite their king-pins having previously been taken out of circulation. The appearance in Tudlinghall of drug-taking paraphernalia on the village green, and to everyone's consternation, on the school playing field, as well as on the memorial hall playing field, was now uppermost in everyone's mind, not just the Police.

Miss Walsh met Sandra on Church Plain, just coming out of Hank's. Although the shop had been renamed Victoria Stores on being sold, it remained firmly Hank's in Miss Walsh's mind, and in the conversations of the villagers who had known it before.

Sandra made a fuss of Truncheon, and invited Miss Walsh to join her at Dodgers for a cup of tea.

'You remember them papers what I took from my brother's house when you was there with me?' she asked, once they had been served with tea and cake for Miss Walsh, and a sausage roll for Sandra.

Miss Walsh indicated that she did indeed remember them.

'Well, you'll never guess what?' Sandra went on.

Miss Walsh raised her eyebrows and waited.

'I found them divorce papers what Trevor were sent by *her*,' by which Miss Walsh inferred she meant Tish. 'And he had signed them after all!'

'Goodness!' Miss Walsh said, feeling she ought to make some verbal contribution this time.

'Yes, and what's more, I sent 'em back,' Sandra said in triumph. 'So that means they are divorced, and she don't get nothing from his estate.'

Although by no means an expert on divorce law, Miss Walsh was almost certain that this was not the case, but decided to let Sandra find that out for herself.

'And you'll never guess what else?' Sandra said, leaning forward to speak more confidentially. 'I also found my parents' Will and I didn't know this but they left the house to me and Trevor together!'

'Oh!' Miss Walsh said, genuinely surprised by this. 'I thought you said they'd left it to your brother because he looked after them?'

'That's what I thought too,' Sandra said, 'But they left it half to each of us and Trevor's left it all to me now.'

'In that case ...' Miss Walsh said slowly, trying to work it out, 'If Tish makes a claim which is upheld for half of Trevor's assets, she's entitled to a quarter of the house.'

'That cow!' Sandra hissed loudly, causing several people on other tables to look around. She leaned forward even further. 'What can I do about that?'

'Well, your solicitor will advise you, but I'd say you could perhaps offer to buy her out if you can?'

'What if she refuse?'

'I've no idea. I suppose if you sell it, she'd be entitled to a quarter.'

The two women sat in silence for a moment, drinking their tea, and Sandra dropping flakes of her sausage roll down for Truncheon.

'Did you spend much time with your brother?' Miss Walsh asked.

'Not really. He'd come for Sunday dinner most weeks, but we were both busy rest of the week at work.'

'And how was he in the weeks before his death? Did you notice any changes in his behaviour, or did he mention he wasn't feeling well, or anything?'

'No, not really,' Sandra said thoughtfully. 'There were one thing I were surprised about.'

'What was that?'

'He were happier than usual, he were a grumpy old sod, he were, but just before he died he seemed really happy for once.'

'Have you any idea why?'

'Dan say to him what's up with you? And he say he's onto a nice little earner, and he'd be able to buy them expensive tractor parts what he needed to finish off his tractor, and then he were going to ride it to some rally or other and hope to sell it.'

'That's one of the tractors in his back garden?'

'Yes, blummin old things, he were always tinkering about with them.'

'Did he say anything else to you?'

'I were in the kitchen at the time so he were talking to Dan, but I could hear them. Trevor said it were a gift that would keep on giving, and he'd be able to do up the house and all.'

'Goodness! Have you any idea what he was on to that would make him that much money?'

'No,' Sandra said regretfully, 'Dan said to let him in on it, and they both laughed, and that was the last what I saw of him.'

'I'm so sorry, Sandra,' Miss Walsh said, although it didn't seem to her that Trevor was such a loss, but he had been Sandra's brother, the only family she had left, and things like that tend to get overlooked in sudden deaths.

'Well, the funeral's eleven on Wednesday in the Church, if you'd like to come?' Sandra said. 'Afterwards at the Memorial Hall again. There'll be food and some music if I can get someone to work that machine what they got there, and an open bar this time, Trevor's paying for it all. Mandy's helping me again.'

'Thank you,' Miss Walsh said, 'I shall certainly attend to pay my respects.'

As she walked back up the road towards her house, Miss Walsh wondered if Trevor had somehow become involved in a new County Lines network which might have sprung up in Tudlinghall; there weren't many ways that someone could get a lot of money very suddenly without taking on another job, after all. At least she now knew that Trevor's body had finally been released, but what she didn't know was that Sandra, fuelled by a desire to prevent Tish having any part in the event, had requested that the funeral director didn't give out any information about the funeral to anyone who asked. Instead, she had been personally inviting people who'd known Trevor to attend the funeral. And she'd got a detailed inventory of Trevor's bank accounts and savings, and had done her level best to spend as much of it as possible on an elaborate funeral and lavish wake, so there'd be very little for Tish, if her bid for a share of his assets was successful.

The police had, of course, informed Tish that Trevor's body had been released, and in accordance with his wishes, that his funeral was being arranged by his sister. Tish had no friends in Tudlinghall, and so she didn't find out when the funeral was being held, although it didn't really matter – the solicitor had assured her that non-attendance at the funeral would not affect her chances of making a claim for spousal support from his estate.

In the meantime, Miss Walsh decided that it was high time for her to launch her own investigation into Trevor's unexpected demise. She had carefully read the Coroner's report, and had noted the detail about the contusion to the back of the head, which could have been caused by being hit very hard. If Trevor had been hit very hard over the back of his head, it could well have led to him losing consciousness, then losing control of the tractor. If so, the intention could well have been to kill him, and it was therefore murder. Or if the intention had been to play a prank on him, or to pay him back for being an arse, then his death was unintended, but it would still be manslaughter.

Either way, Miss Walsh was not entirely convinced that Trevor's death was accidental, and given her track record of solving cases that the police had failed to solve, she decided to carry out her own investigation.

Walking Trunch was a very good cover for poking around on the playing field. If anyone asked her what she was doing, she could say she was looking for his ball – the questioner was not to know that Trunch (almost!) never lost his ball. The pair of them walked slowly down the field on the left-hand side; Trunch seemed to pick up that this was Detection, not Walkies, and sniffed about diligently. It was still evident where the tractor had gone into the ditch, largely because the ground had been completely churned up by all the vehicles and feet which had concentrated in that area. The police had done a very thorough litter-pick, so there was nothing floating in the ditch any more – really, there was nothing to be seen at all any more. It was most disappointing. Clearly, the investigation would have to take quite a different format.

CHAPTER THIRTEEN: MISS WALSH RE-OPENS THE CASE

Back home, Miss Walsh sat down with a pen and paper to summarise what she knew so far, and what she wanted to find out next. She always discussed everything with Truncheon, and his insights were often invaluable, although on this occasion he had chosen to snooze in front of the fire, instead of paying proper attention. Miss Walsh wondered briefly if that meant Trunch had accepted the findings of the Coroner, and thought there was nothing left to investigate.

'You might be convinced, but I'm not, Trunch,' she said, causing him to prick his ears up and open one eye to look at her. 'The Coroner didn't explain that contusion to the back of his head, but at least didn't ignore it. It could have been caused by the tractor falling on him, or it could have been inflicted prior to the tractor going in to the ditch. That's what we've got to find out, Trunch. Who was there on the morning of his death; how did they hit him on the back of the head, and what with?'

Truncheon gave a sigh, stood up and walked over to the table to rest his chin on her knee, and look intelligently up at her.

'First of all, I think we need to track down the person who found him, and the gender-confused woman with the scatty dog that we met that morning.'

She scanned through the Coroner's report again to see if there was a note of the dog-walker's name. 'No name given; it just says he was found by a dog walker. Hmm, do you think that could be the woman we met, Trunch, and not two separate people?'

Trunch considered it a distinct possibility, and shifted his chin slightly to indicate agreement.

'I think we need to call on Elizabeth at the Grange soon: after all, her boundary runs along that side of the field where he was found.'

Trunch gave a small whine, and Miss Walsh patted him absent-mindedly on the head.

'I know you don't need another walkies today, and it's pretty horrible out there,' she said, 'So how about tomorrow morning we step out and deliver some *Village News* and that'll give us an excuse to knock on doors and see if we can find this dog-walking woman. She won't have had a copy of the latest one if she's only just moved in, and I can welcome her to the village and see if she needs any help with accessing services, or joining clubs or whatever. Then we'll call on Elizabeth.'

With a plan of action in place, Miss Walsh filed her paper under 'F' for 'Fish' and the rest of the evening was spent in their usual pursuits.

The following day was drizzly and grey, and Miss Walsh thought she was more likely to be invited in on such a miserable day than if it had been warm and sunny. She carefully stowed several copies of the last edition of *Village News* in a plastic wallet inside a large shoulder bag, and set off, raincoat, boots, and Truncheon by her side. He was not wearing a raincoat, as Miss Walsh considered that dogs had existed for millennia without coats, and had perfectly serviceable water-proof coats of their own anyway. Truncheon was quite glad, as he thought other dogs wearing coats looked ridiculous.

Discounting all the houses down West Green whose occupants she knew, Miss Walsh knocked firmly on the next one she came to, and was gratified by the accuracy of her guess when the woman she'd met briefly on the morning of Trevor's murder opened the door.

'Can I help you?' the woman said.

Miss Walsh pushed her hood back in the hopes the woman would recognise her, but she clearly didn't.

'We met on the playing field a while back?' she said, 'On a very foggy morning?'

The other woman still looked blank, so Miss Walsh gamely ploughed on with her semi-fiction.

'My name's Leonie Walsh,' she said, 'I'm one of your neighbours, I live a few houses further up.'

It was a not-very-subtle hint that the woman should invite her in, but she still looked blank.

In desperation Miss Walsh played her final card; 'I've brought you a copy of the Parish Magazine,' she said, 'But I don't want it to get wet ...'

Finally, the woman seemed to realise she was angling to be let in.

'Is the dog all right outside?' she asked, 'Only I'm allergic.'

Miss Walsh looked around and spotted a large tree on the boundary with Mr and Mrs Newsome's garden, and trudged over to tell Trunch to stay. 'I won't be long, boy,' she said to him quietly, 'But it's a bit odd that she's allergic if we met her walking a dog.'

For a split second she wondered if she was mistaken in her identification of the woman, but now that she had pretty much forced her way in to the woman's house, she had to go ahead with the small deception about delivering the *Village News*. She trudged back across the gravel, and stepped in through the front door.

'Shall I leave my coat and boots here?' she asked, gesturing at the tiny porch area.

'If you don't mind,' the woman said, 'Come through here, it's warmer.'

Miss Walsh walked through to a small sitting room which was quite sparsely furnished, with one sofa, one armchair, a modern wall-mounted flat-screen television, and an old-fashioned glass-fronted cabinet with shelves.

The woman was still standing and looking at her expectantly, so Miss Walsh delved in her bag and brought out the copies of the magazine.

'This is our parish magazine,' she said, 'Have you seen a copy yet?'

'No, I've only been here a few weeks,' the woman said.

Miss Walsh handed one over and stowed the others back in her bag.

'This is last month's,' the woman said, looking at the cover.

'Yes, I'm sorry if you didn't get one through the door,' Miss Walsh said, 'But that's the latest one. There'll be another one out in a couple of months' time, and I'll make sure you get one this time.'

'Thank you,' the woman said, 'Now, if that's all?'

It was a very definite hint that Miss Walsh should leave, and as she turned towards the door, she turned casually and said, 'I don't think I got your name?'

'That's cos I never told you it,' the woman said, very rudely.

'Well, welcome to Tudlinghall, even if it is a bit belated,' Miss Walsh said. 'Did you move here for work?'

'My daughter and grand-son live here,' the woman said, 'I'm not working at the moment.'

'Oh that's lovely,' Miss Walsh said, a little too heartily, but really the woman was being very cold and unfriendly, and it seemed to be spurring her into jollity as though to compensate.

A mobile phone started ringing, and the woman pulled it out of her pocket, glanced at it and said, 'Oh, excuse me a moment, I have to get that.'

She left the room holding the phone to her ear and saying, 'Just a minute ..' and shut the door behind her.

Left alone, Miss Walsh seized this golden opportunity to go and look through the glass doors of the cabinet. It too was rather sparsely occupied, containing some cricket trophies with the name 'H Taylor' and dates ranging from 1981 – 1990 engraved on them, and a few books mostly by the winning authors of the Richard and Judy book club over the past few years. There was an envelope discarded in a bin, addressed to 'Ms Kylie Cooper, 46 Round Stone Way, Cirencester'.

The door opened and the woman came back in, tucking the phone back into her pocket.

'Didn't you have a dog when we met on the playing field?' Miss Walsh asked, 'A Golden Retriever called 'Bella'?'

'No, I told you I'm allergic,' the woman said, 'I don't remember seeing you before ever. Thank you for bringing the magazine, but I've got to go out now.'

Miss Walsh put her boots and raingear back on in the porch and stepped out in to the rain. The door banged shut behind her without another word from the occupant. Truncheon was sitting patiently under the tree, and she said, 'I'm sorry you had to sit out here, boy,' as she picked up his lead and they set off out of the driveway.

'That was very odd, Trunch,' Miss Walsh continued as they made their way down West Green to where New Lane branched off, almost opposite Thonn's Lane. 'She wouldn't give me her name, but I saw an envelope with a name on, which I assume is her name, and possibly a previous address. Now, where shall we go next?' She decided to continue down West Green so she could keep an eye on the house; if Kylie Cooper did drive or walk out of her front door, Miss Walsh would be well placed to see her leave, and could pretend to still be delivering magazines should Ms Cooper spot her.

They walked backwards and forwards in the increasing drizzle for half an hour, but no-one came out of the house. They walked back up West Green past Kylie Cooper's house again, but there was no sign of her, and the house looked dark and unlived in.

'I don't know, Trunch,' Miss Walsh said, as they dried off by the fire in their own sitting room, 'Have I got it wrong? I'm certain it was her we met on the playing field, although she was all muffled up, but she said she'd never met me before. And the woman we met on the field had a dog, but the woman in that house said she didn't have a dog, and was allergic! Well, I don't want to go out again today, I don't know about you, but let's leave Elizabeth until tomorrow, shall we?'

The following day brought no further illumination, although the weather was much nicer, and there was a little warmth in the sun. They walked slowly past Kylie Cooper's house, but it remained mute. They had the playing field all to themselves, and Miss Walsh threw the ball for Trunch over and over, without really paying much attention; she was attempting to recreate that foggy morning in her own mind. No matter how she thought about it, she remained convinced that the woman with the male dog she'd called 'Bella' was definitely the unfriendly woman she'd met the previous day.

On their return home, they were surprised to see a police car in the driveway, and as they approached, a female uniformed officer stepped out of the driver's door.

'Hello, Miss Walsh,' PC Jan Rivers said, 'Are you free for a chat?'

CHAPTER FOURTEEN: MISS WALSH IS PUZZLED

'Yes, of course!' Miss Walsh said, 'Do please come in.'

'Is this your ex-police dog?' Jan asked, 'He's very handsome.'

'And doesn't he know it!' Miss Walsh said, as she unlocked the door and ushered Jan in.

Once they were settled in the sitting room by the fire, with cups of tea, Miss Walsh turned to Jan and said, 'What can I do for you?'

'I'm sorry I wasn't able to call in and see you before the inquest into the caretaker's death, but wanted to thank you for your help with the widow at the solicitor's office.'

'You're welcome,' Miss Walsh said, and then hesitated before asking, 'Am I right in thinking that his body was found by a dog walker who lives somewhere locally?'

'Yes, that's right,' Jan said, 'but she's asked not to be identified, so I'm afraid I can't give you her name. Anyway, that case is all wrapped up now, what I wanted to come and talk to you about was there have been reports of drug-taking paraphernalia being found by villagers around Tudlinghall. Have you seen or heard anything about this?'

'A bit,' Miss Walsh said, 'The kids usually smoke a bit of weed on the playing field or the school field. I can't say I've actually seen any harder drugs being peddled, although I have heard that they are being used in the village. I can certainly keep my ear to the ground and let you know if I do hear anything.'

'That would be very helpful, thank you,' Jan said. 'We can't be here all the time, and people tend to behave differently when they see us, but you are a resident and might be able to pass a bit more unnoticed, but please don't take any risks, they are ruthless people.'

They chatted a bit more, and Jan made a fuss of Truncheon, who accepted it as his due, and then she left, but not before Miss Walsh said, 'Are you and DS Whitaker happy with the outcome of the Inquest into Trevor Fish?'

'Oh yes,' Jan said, 'There's no doubt at all that it was a tragic accident, although, as the Coroner said, he could have taken better care of his health, and his tractor.'

'I see, thank you,' Miss Walsh said, and waved Jan off in her car.

'No doubt at all, Trunch, eh?' she said, returning to the sitting room, 'I'd say there was plenty of doubt. And, I don't know if she meant to let it slip or not, but we now know the dog walker who found his body was a woman, which makes me even more sure it's our Ms Kylie Cooper. Right, let's have some lunch, and then you're coming with me to the Grange.'

It wasn't far to walk up to Tudlinghall Grange (known to villagers as 'the Grange'), but the pavement stopped half way, so they had to walk along the road, and Trunch stayed very smartly to heel until they turned in at the gates, then Miss Walsh gave him the signal, and he rushed off into the woodlands to one side of the main driveway. Miss Walsh had recently made friends with the owners after joining Elizabeth's monthly afternoon book group, and hoped they wouldn't mind Trunch exploring, but she knew he'd come straight back if she called him anyway.

By the time she reached the open lawned area in front of the main house, she could see Trunch had found Elizabeth and was rolling over on his back to have his tummy tickled.

'Hello!' she called, striding up to them both.

'Oh hello Leonie!' Elizabeth said, standing up again. She was dressed for gardening, and had made considerable inroads into one of the flower-beds. 'I was hoping this dog hadn't come in all on his own. Is he yours?'

'Yes, sorry, this is Truncheon,' Miss Walsh said.

'What a marvellous name for a dog! Was he a police dog?'

'He was indeed,' Miss Walsh said.

'Did you work with him?'

'No, he was retiring at around the same time as me, so we took each other on,' Miss Walsh explained.

'How lovely, well, I'm pleased to meet him, and I'm glad you've come, I'm gasping for a cup of tea, and you are a very good excuse to stop work.'

'I'm always glad to be a good excuse to stop work,' Miss Walsh laughed and they walked companionably towards the house, but instead of branching off to the annexe, Elizabeth made her way round to the right of the house, and to the main kitchen door.

'I got back a couple of days ago,' she said, 'but my son hasn't come back yet, so I just need to check the dogs, and then we may as well have a cup of tea here as well, rather than go round to the annexe. It's nice enough to sit out on the terrace today.'

'Do you want me to leave Trunch outside?' Miss Walsh asked.

'Oh no, they're very friendly dogs, very relaxed,' Elizabeth said, 'I think they'd ignore a burglar if one got in, not much disturbs their naps.'

There were two big Goldies curled up in baskets in the large kitchen, and Miss Walsh looked closely at them as the sound of Trunch's claws on the tiled floor caused them both to look up, and then get up to engage in some group sniffing.

'I've never had the chance to meet your dogs before,' she said as Elizabeth busied herself with finding cups and filling the kettle.

'Oh that's because of Joyce,' Elizabeth said, 'She's terrified of dogs, even great softies like these, so I tell my son to keep them shut away when you all come for book-group. Even though we meet in the annexe, they're so used to running in and out wherever they please, and I don't want Joyce to stop coming because of the dogs.'

As if to demonstrate their ability to go where they pleased, all three dogs rushed out through the back door to chase each other about the extensive grounds, barking with glee.

'Well, that's good,' Elizabeth said, looking round pleased, 'That's the most exercise they've had since I got home, and means I won't have to try and get them to go for a walk later.'

'What are their names?' Miss Walsh asked.

'The older dog is Paarl, and Durban is her son,' Elizabeth said, smiling out through the window, where Durban and Trunch were chasing each other wildly and Paarl was pottering along behind them, not keeping up at all.

'You've named them after places in South Africa?'

'Yes, they're all places we knew well before we moved over here.'

'I'm sure I saw Durban on the playing field a while back, with a woman I didn't recognise,' Miss Walsh said.

'That was probably our house-sitter,' Elizabeth said, 'Although why she'd be on the playing field when we've got lots of room here for him to run about, I don't know. Maybe she wanted a change of scene.'

'Oh, I didn't realise you'd been away,' Miss Walsh said, in invitation for Elizabeth to tell her all about it.

'Yes, I left just after the last book group meeting, but I don't think I mentioned I was going, there was so much else to talk about. My son took me to Portugal, and so we got a house-sitter in to look after the dogs mostly,' Elizabeth said.

'How lovely, so you have the same person each time?'

'Usually we do, but this time our usual woman wasn't available, and they sent someone else,' Elizabeth said casually.

'And did you meet her before you left?'

'Yes, she came the night before we left, and was very nice. She got on really well with the dogs, and we use a very reputable agency who vets all their sitters really thoroughly, so I never have any concerns.'

'Do you have a leaflet for the agency?' Miss Walsh asked, and Elizabeth rummaged in a drawer and produced a glossy brochure, at the top of which she'd written 'Angela Fawkes'. Miss Walsh smiled a little at the name, and asked if she were an older woman, who she expected would be more responsible, but Elizabeth said, 'Oh no, she was quite a young woman, in her thirties, I'd say, but very sensible and competent, and I would recommend her. There wasn't a speck of dust anywhere when I came home, and the dogs seemed perfectly happy and well looked after.'

While Elizabeth was distracted by the business of tea-making, Miss Walsh hastily photographed the front of the brochure to capture the agency's phone number and the house-sitter's name, and then turned her attention back to her hostess and her account of her stay in Portugal with her son and his family.

'Now we've only got a couple of days till the next book group meeting,' Elizabeth said when Miss Walsh stood up to leave, 'How did you get on with this month's book?'

'No spoilers!' Miss Walsh replied, wagging her finger, and they both laughed.

CHAPTER FIFTEEN – CURIOUSER AND CURIOUSER

'Well, Trunch,' Miss Walsh said as they made their way sedately back down West Green, 'It's all getting curiouser and curiouser. The woman I saw with Durban was definitely the woman who's now calling herself Kylie Cooper, not Angela Fawkes. Because I'd say the woman with Durban was around my age, and Elizabeth said Angela Fawkes was a woman in her thirties. Kylie Cooper clearly didn't know Durban's gender, or his name, but why, and how? Why was she walking him if he was in the care of Angela Fawkes at the Grange? And if Kylie knew Angela before she came to house-sit, and borrowed him for walkies; why again? She told me she was allergic to dogs!'

Truncheon had had a really good time with his friends and didn't care one way or the other. He'd managed to charm a biscuit out of Elizabeth while Miss Walsh wasn't looking, so he was perfectly contented with the outcome of the visit, and not at all puzzled by anything. He knew that Durban was the same dog he'd met on the playing field, but there was no way of telling his mistress that, so with perfect philosophical aplomb he dismissed the matter and focused on intelligence gathering on the way back down the road by sniffing pretty much every blade of grass.

Once home, Miss Walsh rang the house-sitting agency, and discovered that they didn't have an agent called Angela Fawkes, and that the usual house-sitter had been contracted to sit for Mrs Harte at Tudlinghall Grange.

'Would she be available to come and house-sit for me?' she next asked, 'As she comes highly recommended by Mrs Harte, who is a friend of mine.'

There were formalities to go through, and Miss Walsh had to come up with some fictitious dates, and then agree to a meeting beforehand with Ms Amelia Frost, who was the usual house-sitter for Mrs Harte.

'I hope she likes dogs,' Miss Walsh said, 'I have a former police dog.'

'And you were intending to leave the dog with the house-sitter?' asked the secretary of the House-sitting agency.

'Yes, I understood that Ms Frost looked after dogs as well as the house?'

'Yes, but obviously we have to ensure that our sitters will be safe with the dog,' the secretary said, 'She's met Mrs Harte's dogs a number of times before, so it's not a problem when she goes to sit there.'

'Oh, of course,' Miss Walsh said, 'Well, I don't know how to reassure you, but my dog is very well trained, and obedient, but maybe Ms Frost would need to meet him and be reassured that she's safe with him?'

'That would be advisable,' the secretary said, 'Now did you have a date in mind to meet Miss Frost, and are you happy for her to come to your house for the meeting?'

They arranged a date for the following week, and Miss Walsh rang off and sat down to try and think things through. Elizabeth had said it wasn't their usual house-sitter who had come, but that she'd met the new woman and been happy that she'd come from the agency, but as far as the agency was concerned, they had sent out the usual woman. Miss Walsh felt as though she were still stumbling about in the fog of that morning when Trevor Fish had been killed, and nothing was becoming any clearer.

Her phone rang and it was Marjorie suggesting a trip into the city the following day.

'Good idea,' Miss Walsh said, 'I need a change of scene. Do you need anything in particular, or just a look around?'

'Beth's sold her house at last, well subject to all the usual things, so I want to have a look at house agent details and see if there's anything suitable in Tudlinghall for her,' Marjorie said.

'Wouldn't town be a better bet for Tudlinghall details?'

'I've already been to there and picked up everything they've got,' Marjorie said, 'I wanted to have a look in the bigger agents in the city, and well, really it's an excuse to get out of the house for a day, and have some lunch in a nice cafe.'

'Is Beth looking online as well?' Miss Walsh asked.

'Oh yes, but I'm being old-school and picking up paper copies for her,' Marjorie said, 'I do find it quite hard to see things properly online and I'm damned if I'm spending money to print the details out when the agencies can do it for me. They've got to earn their fees somehow!'

'True, well, it'll be interesting to see what they've got and how much houses are going for in Tudlinghall these days,' Miss Walsh said, and they agreed a time to meet up and walk down to the main road to catch the bus from opposite the Pharmacy.

Before she went to bed, Miss Walsh fired up her laptop, and searched for 'H Taylor Cricket' on Google. 'H Taylor' turned out to be Helen Taylor, a lesser-known member of the England Cricket Team between 1981 and 1999, usually positioned at Deep Backward or Forward. She was known for the strength and accuracy of her throw, but retired in 1999 due to injury.

'I wonder what relation Helen Taylor is to Kylie Cooper, Trunch?' She asked thoughtfully. 'Sister? Daughter? Friend? Or is Kylie Cooper also known as Helen Taylor?'

There was little information on what Helen Taylor had been doing since she quit professional cricket, just a stub really on Wikipedia, with no photograph. She had coached county cricket for some years, but even that information was around ten years old now. Miss Walsh Googled images of the England Cricket Team between 1981 and 1999, but the players all looked the same, and she couldn't say with any confidence that one of them was definitely Kylie Cooper. They were all photographed in caps with their hair tied back and wearing tracksuits; they all looked very similar, happy young women with smiling faces.

***

'Did you hear the school's been broken into again?' Marjorie asked, as they settled on the bus the following morning.

'Has it? Anything taken?'

'The usual; laptops and TVs, anything they can sell on quickly,' Marjorie said, 'But they left an awful mess and William's class had to be taught in the hall instead while their room was sorted out.'

'Now then, Marjorie,' Miss Walsh said sternly, 'We've discussed this.'

'I know!' wailed Marjorie, 'But I just can't call him ...'

'Rollo,' Miss Walsh said firmly, 'His name is Rollo. William is his middle name.'

'Such a stupid name,' Marjorie huffed, 'He's going to get ripped to shreds at High School. They'll call him 'Rolo' after the sweets.'

'Unusual names are more common these days, if that makes sense,' Miss Walsh said soothingly, 'And by the time Rollo gets to High School they'll all be called what we think of as unusual names, and they'll be teasing children called James instead.'

'Oh I do hope so, the poor little thing,' Marjorie said.

'Did Annie tell you about the break-in?' Miss Walsh asked.

'No, she doesn't speak to me if she can avoid it,' Marjorie said, 'It was Will – Rollo who told me when I picked him up after school yesterday. He thought it was all very exciting as they got to do lots of running around and not much learning from what I can gather.'

Miss Walsh thought it was no wonder Marjorie's daughter-in-law avoided her when she'd been so forthright in her condemnation of her children's names, but she had pointed that out before, so decided to focus instead on the break-in.

'I wonder if it's linked to the drugs,' she said thoughtfully.

'Drugs?'

'Yes, the rumours of drug-taking in the village.'

'Oh they're more than rumours,' Marjorie said, 'I know loads of people who've seen needles on the village green, and furtive bodies lurking in bits of woodland round the back of the school.'

'Really?' Miss Walsh said thoughtfully. 'Well, at least I know where to look for a start.'

'Have you been asked to investigate?' Marjorie said excitedly.

'PC Jan Rivers called in and asked me to keep my ear to the ground, but not to put myself into any danger,' Miss Walsh said, 'So I thought I'd have a nosy around during the day; they're not likely to be up to anything illegal during the day.'

'Well, let's hope not,' Marjorie replied. 'I agree with the police-lady, you keep yourself out of trouble.'

The rest of the day was spent very pleasurably in window-shopping, finding a nice café for lunch, and then scouring the estate agents for properties in Tudlinghall and the surrounding villages.

It was in William H Brown on Bank Plain that another piece was added to the puzzle.

'Now, there's this house,' the agent said, somewhat apologetically. 'It's been empty for several years, although we're not sure why. It just needs a little bit of renovation, and the price has been adjusted to allow for work on the roof, installing central heating, and modernisation of the facilities. I would recommend a structural survey on the property as well, but I'm sure that there isn't really any subsidence, and damp is easily dealt with once a property is properly aired and heated. Yes, with a little care, it would be a very nice property indeed, and as Tudlinghall is a popular village this property will be a good investment and will certainly increase in value. These are the details for you.'

Marjorie was nodding intelligently, but Miss Walsh wasn't listening. The house on the details being held before her was the house she had visited to see Ms Kylie Cooper!

'Excuse me,' she interrupted the flow of words all intended to make the house as appealing as possible while doing almost exactly the opposite, 'Did you say this house has been empty for several years?'

'Yes, but I think that just because it hasn't been marketed well by some of our competitors,' the agent said, 'Now that it's been placed with us, we expect to sell it very quickly indeed.'

'So … it hasn't been let out while the owner has been waiting to sell?' Miss Walsh asked.

'No, the owner didn't want to let it out, they want it to be sold.'

'Mrs Howard lived there,' Marjorie said, leaning over to look at the details, 'She died, oh it must be two years ago, and I haven't noticed anyone moving in. There isn't a house agent board outside.'

'We installed one when we put the house on our books,' the agent said.

'Well,' Marjorie said, 'I live along there, and there's nothing up for sale nearby.'

'There should be a board,' the agent said, frowning, 'We haven't negotiated anything with the owner about not having a board outside.'

'We'd like to see this house as soon as possible,' Miss Walsh interrupted firmly. 'This afternoon or tomorrow morning at the latest if you are available.'

'Oh good,' the agent said, looking very pleased indeed, 'I knew you would recognise its value instantly; it's really a very desirable property. Just a moment I'll check the engagements diary.'

While the agent fiddled about with the online engagements diary, Marjorie stared in silent surprise at her friend. Miss Walsh mouthed, 'Tell you later', and she nodded back.

'Ah, here we are,' the agent said, 'Marie Young lives in Tudlinghall, so I'll ask her if she'd mind giving you a quick preliminary look at the house after work today, and if you like it, which I'm sure you will, she can then arrange a proper viewing tomorrow or the next day; how does that sound?'

'Excellent, thank you,' Miss Walsh said, and practically dragged Marjorie out of the office so that they could catch the next bus home to coincide with Ms Young's arrival after work that afternoon. It would take the bus a lot longer to get back to Tudlinghall than it would Ms Young, and then they had to walk up from the bus stop as well to rendezvous with her at the property.

CHAPTER SIXTEEN: COLLECTING MORE PIECES

'What was all that about?' Marjorie asked, as they secured their seats on the bus home. 'Why do we have to see that house right now?'

Miss Walsh looked around and then lowered her head and her voice so that Marjorie had to bend forward as well to hear her, as she fished the details out of her handbag and waved it at her friend.

'Mrs Howard's house is where I went and found that woman I saw with the dog on the day that man died,' she whispered, 'She was in there, but the agent said it wasn't rented out, and she clearly hasn't bought it as it's still on the market!'

'Oh!' Marjorie whispered back, 'I see, so you want to go inside and look for clues?'

'Yes,' Miss Walsh said, 'I thought it was a bit odd at the time, it didn't really look like she was living there. There was very little furniture in the room I saw, and she was desperate to get me out as quickly as possible. I suspect she was cuckooing.'

'Cuckooing?' echoed Marjorie.

'Well, not exactly cuckooing in the modern sense,' Miss Walsh conceded, 'There's no vulnerable person living there for her to move in on, and I don't know if she's connected with the outbreak of drug-taking in the village anyway. But she may well be a cuckoo in the original sense of the word, meaning that she's moved into someone else's nest and is using it as her own. Whatever the truth of it is, she shouldn't be in that house, and therefore she must be up to no good.'

'How exciting!' Marjorie said, slightly too loudly, 'Am I detecting with you now?'

Miss Walsh shushed her gently and then said, 'Yes, you can be my Doctor Watson, if you like!'

Marjorie shuddered with pleasurable anticipation, and smiled broadly for the rest of the journey back to Tudlinghall.

The bus stopped opposite the Pharmacy and they got off and started heading up to Church Plain when Marjorie suddenly stopped and clutched Miss Walsh's arm.

'What if she's there?' she asked.

'Who? The house agent? I hope so, or we can't get in.'

'No, that woman. What if she's still in there, being a cuckoo?'

'Oh, I hadn't thought of that. Well, she'll be caught out won't she, when we turn up with official permission to view the house. Don't worry, I don't suppose she'd be violent.'

As they panted up the road towards the vacant house to meet Ms Young, they could see a car had pulled into the driveway, and a young woman, smartly dressed and in high heels was rooting around in the overgrown front flowerbed. She stood up, holding a William H Brown 'For Sale' sign mounted on a stout stake, and propped it up against the fence at the front.

'Kylie Cooper took the 'For Sale' sign down,' Miss Walsh said to Marjorie, 'No wonder you didn't know it was for sale!'

'Very naughty,' Marjorie said.

'Ms Young?' Miss Walsh called as they got within ear-shot.

The young woman waved, and walked away from the sign, brushing dirt off her hands as she did so.

'I'm sorry, I can't shake hands,' she said as the two older women arrived. 'I'm all muddy, but I'll wash my hands inside. Perhaps you would unlock the front door for me?'

She handed Marjorie a set of keys, but they didn't open the front door, and Marjorie handed them back to her.

'She's had the locks changed!' Miss Walsh said, and walked to the front window to peer through. 'I can't see anyone,' she said, but from what she could see, the sofa, chair and glass-fronted cabinet were still there, although the latter was empty of trophies and books now.

'Looks like she's gone,' she said.

'Who's gone?' the estate agent asked, peering at the bunch of keys in the fading light. 'Oh, the owner hasn't ever lived here, they inherited it and are selling it. Maybe George gave me the wrong keys, but no, here's the address.' She showed them a key-fob with the address on. It was the right address, but the keys didn't work in the front door lock.

'Can we get around the back?' Miss Walsh asked, her detective instincts aroused.

The three women walked to the left of the bungalow and around it, with Miss Walsh in the lead, pushing through the very long grass. It didn't look as though anyone had been into or out of the back garden for a long time, but the back door was equally locked tight, and the key didn't work there either.

'Well,' the estate agent said, as they waded back to the driveway again. 'I'm very sorry, I'll have to contact the owners and ask if they've changed the locks, and get some new keys from them. If you could give me a few days and then contact the office, we'll make an appointment to come and view the property again.'

'Thank you very much,' Marjorie said warmly, tucking Ms Young's card into her pocket. 'I'll certainly do that. I've got the details here and I'll pass them on to my daughter, and maybe by the time you've sorted out the keys, she'll be able to come and see the house too.'

'That would be great,' Ms Young said. 'Thank you both for coming and I'm very sorry we haven't been able to gain access. Now, can I offer you a lift home? It's suddenly very dark.'

'Oh that's all right, thank you,' Marjorie said, 'We both live just a few more doors down.'

They watched Ms Young drive away and then Miss Walsh opened up the wheelie bin lid and started looking inside.

'What are you doing?' Marjorie asked, 'Oh, are you detecting?'

'Yes,' Miss Walsh said, 'She might have put something in the bin which would give us a clue about where she's gone.'

But it seemed Kylie Cooper was too careful, and the bin was empty. Disappointed, the two women set off up West Green towards their own homes.

'Well, I do think Beth might like it,' Marjorie said as they reached her house, 'I know you weren't thinking of Beth when you asked to look around, but she is looking for something in Tudlinghall, and this is a much lower price than the other houses I've got details for.'

'It needs a lot of work,' Miss Walsh said, vaguely.

'Yes, but Beth won't mind that. Now would you like to come in for a cuppa?' Marjorie asked, but Miss Walsh said she'd left Trunch all day, and he'd need to be let out and fed, so she'd better get back.

Trunch had indeed been crossing his legs until she got back, and Miss Walsh let him out into the garden to relieve himself. He sniffed about a bit, but there wasn't much news in his own back yard, so he soon came back in again.

'Do you mind if we don't go out for walkies this evening, Trunch?' Miss Walsh asked, as she prepared his supper. 'It's been quite a long day and I've got to brace myself for hearing the children read at the school tomorrow.'

Trunch swallowed his supper in seconds and went to lie down in front of the fire in tacit agreement that he didn't expect walkies that evening.

'We'll go out first thing,' Miss Walsh promised, as she heated a bowl of soup for herself, 'And I'll be back lunch time, so we can go out again then, if you want.'

She added more notes to the file she'd opened for the drug-taking in the village, and went to bed early.

CHAPTER SEVENTEEN: MISS WALSH DETECTS

A brisk walkies in the early morning light, a nourishing breakfast for them both, and then Miss Walsh set off for Tudlinghall Primary School, on the main road, and her self-inflicted penance of hearing the children read. When she arrived, she was pleased to see that she'd been assigned to Marjorie's daughter-in-law's class, which meant she'd be able to ask her more about the break-in, and if the staff had any knowledge of the drug-taking that was alleged to be happening at the end of their field.

Annie Ward knew that Miss Walsh was a friend of her mother-in-law and was consequently a little formal towards her, but as they conferred over which children would benefit most from Miss Walsh's help, she did unbend a bit and told Miss Walsh about the break-in.

'It's usually carried out by children who came here themselves, and still live in the village,' she said. 'I don't know what happens to them once they get to Secondary school, but maybe it's hormones or something. Anyway, the police came and investigated, but we haven't heard anything. I expect the things they stole are all on e-bay by now, but it leaves us without tablets for some of the special needs children who use them. We have re-ordered, but it takes time, and then they've got to be programmed for their specific needs. It's a bit of a nightmare really.'

'Have you seen any evidence of drug-taking on the school field?' Miss Walsh asked.

'Yes, we can't let the children out to play until the field has been checked, and all the needles and other stuff picked up off the grass, it's awful.'

'Whereabouts is all the stuff?'

'Right down the bottom of the field, where it backs on to the little bit of woodland and the footpath. The fence has been broken down there, and there's no money to mend it, so they're getting in there.'

At the end of a long morning listening to children stumbling over simple words in their reading books at a pace which was like a monotonous hypnotic chant, Miss Walsh decided she needed fresh air to wake herself up a bit, and offered to join the team who were heading out to clear the field while the children had their lunch. The caretaker, the groundsman, two parent volunteers and a teacher who wasn't on lunch duty were all standing out in the playground being briefed by the caretaker who had been trained by the police in how to clear the paraphernalia safely. He issued her with a hi-vis jacket, a pair of gloves, a litter pick-up stick, and a reinforced bag.

'Do you have to do this every day?' Miss Walsh asked the teacher as they set off across the field.

'Yes,' he replied grimly, 'We don't dare let the children out to play until we're sure there's nothing more dangerous on the field than the crows, and the dinner ladies.'

At the end of the field, they each moved to their designated areas and went over them very carefully, using the pick-up sticks to part any longer grasses and to pick up the things they found. There wasn't very much in the end, but quite enough to have posed a considerable hazard to any child who had come across them.

'We've done assemblies on this,' the teacher said to Miss Walsh as they trudged back across the field to dispose of their finds, 'We've told the children time and again not to touch anything they see in the grass, but to go and fetch a teacher or a lunch time supervisor, but you know what children are.'

'Indeed,' Miss Walsh said.

She disposed of her bag of finds in the bin that had been provided by the police, and then said she'd like to go back down the field and walk around the footpath to get home. The fence at the bottom of the field had been broken down, so egress was easy, and she climbed over being very vigilant for any needles which were outside the school field, and had therefore not been cleared.

There was a lovely clearing in the trees, which was ruined by dog-poo bags, cans, cigarette packets, crisp packets, and other litter. Logs had been pulled into a rough circle and there was evidence that someone had been lighting a bonfire here; possibly the same people who were taking the drugs, and there were needles and spoons scattered around the logs and in the bonfire.

As Miss Walsh continued up the footpath which led around the side of the school field, she could see other places where the fence had been broken down, and lots more evidence that some people carried lots of one-use-plastic food-and-drink items with them whenever they went out into the countryside. These same people apparently had not worked out what a bin was for and just discarded the plastic as soon as they'd consumed the contents. The path was well-trodden, but there was no more evidence of drug-taking that she could see.

As she continued around the back of the new houses on School Plain and emerged onto Church Plain, Miss Walsh decided that she would have to go back at night and hope to find some people engaged in drug-taking.

***

Miss Walsh's meeting with the house-sitter was remarkable in that it didn't take place at all, but that it did add some vital information to the puzzle she was assembling. A car arrived in her drive-way at the time appointed for Ms Amelia Frost, and a woman climbed out, looking serious. Miss Walsh was waiting in the doorway and called out, 'Ms Frost? Do come in.'

The woman followed Miss Walsh into the sitting room, where Trunch was on his best and most winsome behaviour, sitting neatly on the hearth-rug.

'What a gorgeous dog!' the woman said, and Trunch wagged his tail and did all he could to look well-behaved and unthreatening as instructed. 'But I'm sorry to have to tell you that Amelia Frost is no longer working for our agency; my name is Anne Perry, and I'm the owner of 'Home First', the house-sitting agency. Here is my identification, and I'm happy for you to ring the office to check on me, as well.'

'Oh!' Miss Walsh said, surprised. 'Thank you, but I'm happy you are who you say you are. Please do sit down, can I get you a tea or coffee?'

'No thank you,' Anne Perry said, 'I'm afraid that what I have to tell you does not reflect well on our agency at all, but that I will guarantee you a week's free house-sitting at any time of your choosing as a good-will gesture. I have done the same for Mrs Harte.'

'Why? Whatever has happened?' Miss Walsh asked.

Anne Perry gathered her thoughts and explained that Amelia Frost had been one of their most trusted and valued employees at 'Home First', and they had been happy to send her to Mrs Harte to house-sit at Tudlinghall Grange whenever she was available. However, on this last occasion, without telling 'Home First', Amelia didn't turn up for the sit. Instead, another woman calling herself Angela Fawkes arrived for the pre-sit meeting with Mrs Harte and convinced her that she'd come from the agency, instead of Amelia; and that the agency knew all about it. Unfortunately, Mrs Harte didn't check with 'Home First', and the sit went ahead with Angela Fawkes. Luckily nothing seemed to have gone wrong, but the agency really had no idea why Amelia let Angela take her place.

'My goodness! What a deception!' Miss Walsh said, 'How did you find out?'

'Mrs Harte filled in our after-sit feed-back form, in which she said she had been sorry that Amelia had been unavailable this time, but that she'd been very happy with someone called Angela Fawkes. Of course, we didn't have any such person on our books, and then my receptionist told me that you'd also requested this Angela Fawkes, and I realised something had gone badly wrong.'

'How extraordinary!' said Miss Walsh. 'Did you track Amelia down to find out her side of the story, then?'

'No, unfortunately Amelia was discovered dead in her flat in Peterborough a few weeks ago, and the Police contacted us as we were her most recent employer. They had found emails from someone who appeared to have offered Amelia a job abroad, and reassured her that we knew all about it, although when the Police attempted to trace the emails, there was no such person or job, of course.'

'Do you happen to know the name of the person who emailed Amelia?' Miss Walsh asked.

'Well, I'm not sure ... '

'If it helps, I'm a retired Police Inspector, hence the retired police dog there,' Miss Walsh said nodding at Trunch.

'Well, in that case, the police told me that the person who contacted Amelia was called Kelly Cooper, I think it was, and she claimed to be the manager of a company called 'Mi Casa, Tu Casa'. There is a website, and everything, but the police say it's all fraudulent, and there is no such organisation in Spain. They've been unable to trace this Kelly Cooper either.'

'Ah,' Miss Walsh said, 'In that case, I might have some helpful information for the police, which may help them to trace her.'

'Do you know her?' Anne asked, startled.

'Not exactly, but I believe she was resident in this village until a few days ago. Leave it with me, and I'll let the police know.'

'Very well,' Anne said, 'I won't take up any more of your time, but here is my card with a reference number on it, and if you would like one of our house-sitters to come and look after your house and dog, you can have a week for free.'

'Thank you,' Miss Walsh said, and waited until she'd driven away before returning to update Truncheon. 'Wheels within wheels, Trunch, but all the threads are joining up, if I may mix my metaphors. I'm sure that Kelly Cooper and Kylie Cooper are one and the same person. Now why did Angela Fawkes and Kylie Cooper need to keep Amelia Frost out of Tudlinghall? Why were they both here at the same time? I think we are going to need a night expedition, boy; better brush up on your camouflage, and engage stealth mode.'

AMELIA'S STORY - COLLATERAL DAMAGE

Amelia took a deep breath of delight when the job offer confirmation email from 'Mi Casa, Tu Casa' dropped into her email account. It felt like months since she'd first sent in her application to them, and this was more important to her than anything she'd ever done before. These intervening months had felt like a particular form of torture now that she'd got the promise of a better life, and her tiny studio flat in a run-down area of Peterborough felt even more constricting than ever.

The weather hadn't helped either; months of a damp and cold English Autumn and Winter, months passing while she was missing out on the warmth and glamour of a villa in the south of Spain. She couldn't wait for the end of her dismal life of drudgery in dreary old England; she could almost taste the Sangria!

It wasn't that she hadn't enjoyed the house-sitting; she had. It was very enjoyable to stay in gorgeous houses like Tudlinghall Grange, and pretend for a few weeks that she was a wealthy woman; the Lady of this Manor. There were long periods in between sits, however, and then she was stuck trying to make the money stretch until the next house-sit; she didn't want to take a job in a supermarket because if another house-sit came up, she might not be available. And all the time, her desire to travel, to better herself, was so strong.

She'd searched online for a company doing house-sits for people abroad, and found a job advertised by a company called 'Mi Casa, Tu Casa', but not for a house-sitter. The job was for a manager to arrange the house-sits and manage the sitters in the south of Spain. Amelia couldn't believe her luck. It was a very attractive package; a villa was provided with a housekeeper, a car, generous pay and conditions, a pension. Amelia was delighted when they requested a Zoom interview after she sent in her CV.

The Zoom interview went very well; Amelia dressed as smartly as she could, well from the waist up anyway, and put on full make-up. She made sure to name-drop as many of the rich and posh people she'd house-sat for, and casually dropped in that they all loved her and requested her by name when they needed a house-sitter again. The director, Ms Cooper, said that they had been very impressed by her CV, and asked if she had any sits arranged in the next couple of months, as they would need her to fly out to Spain to see where she would be working, and check that she and the job were suited to one another.

There was only one house-sit coming up; Tudlinghall Grange. That was not at all a problem Ms Cooper said, the director of 'Home First' was a friend of hers, they had worked together in the past, and she would contact 'Home First' to say that Amelia was moving on, and advise them to find a substitute for the sit at Tudlinghall Hall. Really, Amelia was not to worry about a thing, Ms Cooper would sort it all out for her; and get a reference from 'Home First' at the same time, although that would be merely a formality, it was clear that Amelia was exactly what they were looking for.

Dazzled by all of this, and not wanting to do anything to jinx this wonderful opportunity, Amelia didn't contact 'Home First', and didn't do any more investigation into 'Mi Casa, Tu Casa' either. The email which had just pinged into her inbox was from Ms Cooper to say Ann Parry was fine with Amelia leaving the 'Home First', and had provided glowing references, and could Amelia be on stand-by to fly out to Spain within the next few days? They were just working on getting her the appropriate Visa to live and work in Spain; now that we weren't in the EU any more, it was a more lengthy and complicated procedure.

An email came from ann.parry@gmail.com to thank Amelia for all her hard work, and to wish her the very best of luck with her new life and job.

Amelia gave her landlord notice of her departure, sat back, and waited for her new life to begin.

Her body was found a month later when her landlord called in to collect the keys and inventory the flat for new tenants. She had been shot in the head.

CHAPTER EIGHTEEN: NIGHT MANOEUVRES AND MORE INFORMATION

Although she had promised PC Rivers not to engage in any risky behaviour, Miss Walsh decided that she would be perfectly safe with Truncheon – he may have been a retired police dog, but he was still a highly trained police dog, and given the right commands would attack, or defend, or just look menacing enough to keep anyone away from her if necessary.

She dressed in dark clothing; Trunch's fur was very dark, so they should be pretty inconspicuous. She judged that anyone heading for the little clearing with the bonfire would probably go along the footpath from Church Plain, and around the side of the playing field; taking the route she'd walked back from the school field the previous day. It was possible to approach the site from a different direction across the fields, and so she and Truncheon set out down Gwynne's Lane to the footpath across the fields.

It wasn't a particularly dark night, but fog was starting to form in low bands across the fields. Truncheon was alert and very silent, his breath showing in short puffs, while Miss Walsh practiced moving as quietly and without huffing and puffing too much. As they crossed the last field, she could see that the bonfire had been lit, and that there were several people around it already.

Now she just had to get close enough to see and hear without being seen or heard. It wasn't hard; they weren't expecting anyone to be sneaking up on them, and the condition they were in, it was doubtful they'd care even if they did see her.

There wasn't much conversation going on, but two young men were arguing.

'I'll go back and ask her for more, then,' one said.

'She's split,' the second one said.

'Gone?'

'You get your supplies from me now.'

'But you've put the price up.'

'Business my old son. No hard feelings. You just got to sell a bit more, that's all. Probation's over, you're a dealer proper now.'

'No-one told me,' the first voice said sulkily.

Miss Walsh lay down on her front very carefully, and Trunch crouched beside her, on high alert. She focused her night-vision binoculars on the group around the fire, and took some close-up photographs, before getting (with some difficulty) back to her feet, and retreating across the field again.

'Good work, Trunch,' she said once she was certain they were out of earshot of the group in the clearing, 'We've got some great shots of those kids, we can pass on to the police. There's definitely a network being set up here, and I suspect that woman Kylie Cooper is at the bottom of it.'

Trunch agreed, although he was a little disappointed that he hadn't had to chase or bite anyone. They had a celebratory snack and (for Miss Walsh) a sherry, and she finally finished the book for the reading group before going to bed.

The following morning as they returned from walkies, their next-door neighbour, Kathy Berry, stepped out of her driveway to intercept them. Truncheon wagged his tail and smiled ingratiatingly; this human was always good for a tasty treat whenever they met.

'Morning Kathy!' Miss Walsh said, 'How are you today?'

Miss Berry had a long and impressive set of ailments, which she was usually only too happy to talk about, but today she had something else on her mind.

'Good morning to you both too. I was hoping to catch you as you went past; I saw you and Mrs Ward going into Mrs Howard's the other day,' she said, in a lowered voice.

'Yes, Marjorie wanted to see round it for her daughter,' Miss Walsh said, not entirely accurately.

'Oh that would be lovely,' Miss Berry was momentarily diverted from her path by the thought of a friend's daughter returning to Tudlinghall. 'Has she sold her house at last?'

'Subject to contract and chains and all that sort of thing, yes.'

'Well let's keep our fingers crossed for her. But come in and have a cup of tea, I've got a special doggie ice-cream for Truncheon too,' she added as extra inducement, 'They're selling them at the Farm Shop along Wellinghall Road, and I thought of him as soon as I saw them.'

'That's very kind of you,' Miss Walsh said, 'You do spoil him.'

'I don't mind at all, he's such a lovely doggie, such a good boy, aren't you precious?' this to Truncheon, who was wagging his tail in agreement.

Once they were settled in Kathy's kitchen, with cups of tea and wedges of cake for the humans, and a most tasty dog ice-cream for Truncheon, which he chased all round the floor to Kathy's great amusement, she got down to brass tacks.

'Has she moved out, then?'

'Beth? No, she's waiting for it all to go through before she does anything like that. But I expect she could stay with Marjorie and John if the house here isn't ready,' Miss Walsh said.

'No, I meant *her next door*,' Kathy hissed, leaning forward, and casting vicious looks at the wall nearest the house next door.

'Oh, sorry, I thought we were still talking about Beth!' Miss Walsh said with a laugh, 'Yes, as far as I could see through the windows, she's gone. Did you know her at all?'

'No, although it wasn't for want of trying, I can tell you,' Kathy said, sitting up very straight and looking very disapproving.

'Oh, what happened?'

'Well, I went round as soon as I saw her moving in, like we do, and took her one of my lemon drizzle cakes.'

'Your lemon drizzle cakes are the talk of the village,' Miss Walsh said, 'She was lucky it was you who was on duty that week.'

'She didn't want it!'

'No!'

'I knocked on the door and when she answered, I said, 'Welcome to Tudlinghall, my name's Kathy Berry and I live next door. When people move in to our village, we bake them a cake as a welcome. All the churches here take part, and it's my turn this week. I've also brought you a copy of the Methodist church magazine.' She looked at me like I was trying to offer her a doggie poo bag or a used tissue, and said, 'I don't eat cake.' So I said, 'Well, take the magazine then,' and she said, 'I'm not interested in religion,' and shut the door!'

'When was this?' Miss Walsh asked.

'A good month ago,' Kathy said, 'So I went away feeling like, oh I don't know what, just really upset, she was so rude, but by the time I got home I was angry, and suspicious. I thought to myself, she's up to something she doesn't want anyone to know about, so I started keeping an eye on her.'

There was clearly more, so Miss Walsh did her best to look interested but not impatient, and waited.

'First of all, I thought she had her son living with her,' Kathy said. 'She must have been in her late fifties, I'd have guessed, and I saw this boy coming and going who looked to be in his late teens or early twenties.'

Miss Walsh fished in her bag and pulled out her phone onto which she'd downloaded the photos from the night-vision binoculars.

'Did he look like this?' she asked, showing the photo of the two boys who'd been arguing by the fire.

'Yes, that one,' Kathy said, pointing to the one who'd said he was now in control of the supply now that the woman had gone. 'He was in and out of there, and then he started bringing other youngsters with him, some of them I recognised from the village, and others I didn't. I thought they were having sleep-overs, or something.'

'Do you recognise the other boy in this picture?' Miss Walsh asked.

'Yes that's the Savoury boy, isn't it?' Kathy said, peering closely at the photo again. 'Malcolm's grandson?'

'Oh is it, thanks,' Miss Walsh said, 'And what about these others?'

Miss Berry peered at the other photos, and said, 'That's Abbie Milne, that's the little Byatt girl, what's her name? It'll come back to me. Next to her is Ethan Norton, and I think that one's Jack Barratt.'

'How do you know them all?' Miss Walsh asked.

'Youth Club,' Kathy said briefly.

'Do you still run that?'

'No, we got fed up with Trevor Fish messing us about at the Memorial Hall, and it kind of died a death when we couldn't find another suitable venue. Oh! Which reminds me, you'll never guess who else went into that house?'

'I ...no, I really don't know,' Miss Walsh said, 'Malcolm Savoury?'

'No! Trevor Fish!'

Miss Walsh was momentarily stunned. She couldn't think what Trevor might have wanted to go and visit Ms Kylie Cooper for; surely he wasn't a drug addict? Or a pusher?

'I knew that would surprise you!' Miss Kathy said, 'I couldn't believe it either.'

'Do you remember when this was?'

'I do indeed,' Kathy said triumphantly, 'It was two days before he died. Oh! Do you think she had something to do with it?'

'I don't know,' Miss Walsh said, 'But it's certainly a coincidence. Did you tell the police any of this?'

'They didn't ask,' Kathy said. 'Nobody knocked on my door or asked me if I saw anything.'

'Well,' Miss Walsh said, 'I think this is vital evidence, but hang on to it for now. I'm collecting all the pieces together, and I think I might be close to finding out what really did happen to Trevor.'

'You don't think it was an accident, then, like the Inquest said?'

'No, I'm sure it wasn't,' Miss Walsh said.

'How thrilling!' Kathy said, 'And to think I was next door to her all along!'

Kathy Berry insisted on Miss Walsh taking a large portion of the cake home with her, and Truncheon was Extra Good all the way home in the hopes of sharing it with her. Miss Walsh was far too deep in thought to notice his exemplary behaviour.

'Well, Trunch,' she said as they settled into the sitting-room for the evening, 'I think I've got all the pieces now, just need to put together a report of my findings for that nice PC Rivers, and see what happens.'

CHAPTER NINETEEN: MISS WALSH CALLS A MEETING

Writing the report into her investigations took several days, and more than once Miss Walsh doubted her evidence, and double-guessed what the Police might say or do once they received it. Officially Trevor's death had been ruled as an accident, but she thought there was enough new evidence for them to re-open the case.

By the time she finished, Miss Walsh had almost completely lost her nerve. The burn over the Coe case still smarted, and she really didn't want to expose herself to a similar experience over this one. However, she steeled herself after a brisk walk with Truncheon; the police had unofficially asked her to look into the drug-taking in the village, and most of her evidence pertained to that. It was not her fault that Trevor had got himself embroiled in it as well, causing doubt to be cast on the manner of his death.

Before she could change her mind, Miss Walsh made some telephone calls to everyone involved, and set up a coffee morning that they could all make, then she put in a request to Kathy Berry for one of her famous lemon drizzle cakes.

On the morning of the meeting, Kathy Berry arrived first, with her lemon drizzle cake safely stowed in a special cake-carrier.

'Well, this is exciting,' she said, 'Are the police coming?'

'Yes, I hope so. I've invited PC Jan Rivers, as she was the one who asked me to look into the drug-taking in the village,' Miss Walsh replied.

'And to think I've been sitting on vital evidence all this time!' Kathy said, clearly very excited. 'It's just like 'Line of Duty', isn't it?'

Miss Walsh could have told her that 'real' policing was nothing like any of the police-based dramas on the television, but didn't want to burst her bubble. Kathy had indeed provided a vital piece of the puzzle, and what's more made very good cake.

'Do take a seat,' she said, 'I think I can hear a car pulling up, I'll just go to the door.'

'I'll put the kettle on for you,' Kathy said, 'Truncheon will help, won't you boy?'

Truncheon was quite happy to accompany her to the kitchen in hopes of a treat (or two!).

A car had indeed pulled up, containing PC Rivers, and behind it came on foot; Elizabeth Harte, Marjorie Ward, and Sandra Richardson.

Miss Walsh welcomed them all in, got them settled in the sitting room, and said, 'Thank you all for coming; I will introduce you all to each other in a moment, although some of you already know each other, but if I could suggest that I run through what I've discovered about the drug-taking in the village, and then we can discuss it over tea or coffee, and Kathy has provided one of her wonderful cakes.'

'Oh good!' Marjorie and Elizabeth said in unison, and then laughed.

'I think some of you have already met PC Jan Rivers?' Miss Walsh said, 'And to your left is Sandra, Kathy, Elizabeth, and Marjorie. PC Rivers asked me to have a look around to see if I could find out about the reports of drug-taking in Tudlinghall. I have managed to track down where the drugs are being taken,' Miss Walsh went on, 'And I think I know how they got here in the first place, so I'm hopeful that the police will be able to mop up the ring-leaders, and also catch the local contacts. I suspect some of the village children will need some help to get them off the drugs too.'

'Poor things,' Marjorie said, 'How awful for their parents.'

'Indeed,' Miss Walsh said, 'It is a tragedy. As to where it all started, I think I have to go back to when Elizabeth Harte asked her usual house-sitting agency if her usual house-sitter was available, and then a different woman arrived for the pre-sit meeting.'

'Wait a minute,' Jan said, 'Are you Mrs Elizabeth Harte?'

'Yes,' Elizabeth said, rather startled to find she was both the beginning of the mystery and also of sudden interest to the police.

'You're not the woman I met at Tudlinghall Grange who said her name was Liz Harte,' Jan said. 'Do you have a daughter?'

'Yes, I do, but she was on holiday with me in Portugal,' Elizabeth said, 'The woman you met was probably the house-sitter, but I don't know why she said she was me.'

Jan leaned forward, 'Do you have a photograph of your daughter on your phone?' she asked.

'Yes, just a moment,' Elizabeth fished out her phone and started scrolling through it. 'Here she is,' she said, passing it to Jan.

'No, that's definitely not the woman I saw at Tudlinghall Grange,' Jan said. 'What is your daughter's name, please?'

'Donna Ferris.'

'Not Harte?'

'No, she's married.'

'If I may ask, PC Rivers,' Miss Walsh said, 'What did the woman you met at the Grange look like?'

'She was in her thirties I would estimate,' Jan said, 'Average height, with straight shoulder length brown hair cut in a bob, with a fringe, brown eyes, she wore glasses, and had an Essex accent.'

'Well, my daughter's a six-foot curly haired red-head,' Elizabeth said with a laugh, 'And she sounds as South African as me! I think the woman you met was Angela Fawkes, my house-sitter.'

It had never ceased to surprise Miss Walsh that someone as dainty and ash-blonde as Elizabeth could have produced twin children who both topped six feet tall with fiery red hair.

'What on earth is going on?' Marjorie asked.

'I think I have most of the answers,' Miss Walsh said, 'But if could just ask Elizabeth to tell everyone a bit more about the woman called who said she'd come from the house-sitting agency?'

'She said her name was Angela Fawkes, as in Guy Fawkes, and that our usual sitter wasn't available, but she had references and letters from the Agency, and an official badge and everything, so I was perfectly happy.

It's not the first time that our usual woman hasn't been available, so it wasn't a surprise when someone different arrived for the meeting. Although I should have been a bit more wary as I hadn't been notified of the change by the agency in advance, but I'm still not thinking very clearly after Matthew's death.'

Everyone was silent for a moment remembering the awful shock of Matthew's death not that many months before.

'But you found out later that she hadn't come from the agency?' Jan asked.

'That's right,' Elizabeth said, 'The director herself came to see me and was most apologetic. She said she didn't know how it had happened, but they would tighten up all their procedures and it would never happen again.'

'And what was the name of your usual house-sitter?' Jan asked.

'Amelia Frost.'

'Oh!' Jan said.

'Yes,' Miss Walsh said, 'Amelia Frost was unfortunately found murdered in her flat in Peterborough, or so the director of 'Home First' told me.'

Elizabeth pressed her hands to her mouth and everyone looked very shocked.

'I'm afraid that's right,' Jan said, 'Although we don't know who by, it doesn't seem to be linked with the Angela Fawkes who took her place at Tudlinghall Grange.'

'I'm very sorry to have to contradict you,' Miss Walsh said, 'But I think it is linked, and if you are all ok, I'll explain what I've found out.'

CHAPTER TWENTY: THE CASE IS (SORT-OF) SOLVED

'Once I had reassured the director of 'Home First' that I was a retired police inspector, she told me that Amelia Frost had been offered a job abroad by someone called Kelly Cooper, who had also informed her that the agency knew she wouldn't be coming back, and were happy with that. As some of you know, there was a woman called Kylie Cooper living a few doors down the road until very recently. I believe they are one and the same, and that Kelly or Kylie Cooper and Angela Fawkes are jointly responsible for bringing the drugs into Tudlinghall. Angela needed a way to be in the village without any obvious connection with Kylie, and so they worked on getting the usual house-sitter out of the way.'

'But how would they know that Amelia house sat for Elizabeth at the Grange?' Marjorie asked.

'I don't know exactly, but I suspect they did it by advertising a really wonderful sounding job abroad, waited to see who answered the advert, and then moved in on villages or towns where the person had already been employed as a house-sitter. They would promise them a job abroad, get lots of information out of them about the agency they worked for, the people they sat for, and then they would substitute one of their own people. It may be worth seeing if the sudden appearance of drugs in towns and villages is connected in any way with people hiring house-sitters,' Miss Walsh said to Jan.

She was making notes, and nodded.

'I also suspect that Kylie Cooper did the rounds of the estate agents and found a house in Tudlinghall which hadn't sold, managed to get a viewing, and copied the keys. House agents don't always insist on accompanying visits to empty houses these days, and it would be easy for her to get the keys copied. She then changed the locks. It might also be worth asking the local house-agents if they remember giving out keys to a Mrs Kylie or Kelly Cooper for that house just down the road,' Miss Walsh went on.

Jan nodded again.

'After that,' Miss Walsh said regretfully, 'I have no idea how Kylie Cooper recruited the youngsters, but I'm sure it's a slick operation that's played out in towns and cities across England. However, I do have some information on the children she recruited as Kathy saw a young man who wasn't local, and who appeared to be living at her house.'

Kathy beamed around at everyone. 'He was young enough to be her son,' she said, 'and he had lots of friends his own age coming round. I did recognise some of them as local children, including Malcolm Savoury's grandson, Callum.'

Jan made a note of the name and nodded her thanks at Kathy.

'That boy might have been brought to Tudlinghall from somewhere else by Kylie Cooper to make friends with the local youth, start the process of getting them addicted, and then turn them into pushers,' Miss Walsh said.

'Yes,' Jan said, thoughtfully, 'They often traffic a young person into a new area, and then they are given money and drugs to start off their business.'

'I managed to get a photograph of the young man with Malcolm Savoury's grandson at a site where there was a lot of drug-taking paraphernalia,' Miss Walsh said, handing a copy of it to Jan, 'And Kathy has identified the young man on the left there as the one who appeared to be living with Kylie Cooper.'

'Yes, that's him,' Kathy said, leaning over and pointing at the photo in Jan's hand.

'I'll run it through the Missing Persons Register and see if he's disappeared from anywhere,' Jan said. 'Where did you take this photo?'

'In a small bit of woodland at the bottom of the school field,' Miss Walsh said, 'I can take you to it after this meeting, if you like.'

'Thank you. And do you know if this lad is still in Tudlinghall?'

'He was two days ago,' Miss Walsh said, 'Although I've no idea where he's staying. Kylie Cooper seems to have gone, but he might still be in the house.'

'Who are the other children in these pictures?' Jan asked, looking through the print-outs that Miss Walsh had given her.

'I've written the names on the back,' Miss Walsh said.

'That's great, thanks.'

'What's all this got to do with Trev?' Sandra asked suddenly, she'd been sitting very quietly in the presence of The Law, but all of this was completely new to her and she was wondering why Miss Walsh had invited her.

Jan looked up, startled, and Miss Walsh said quickly, 'Sandra is Trevor Fish's sister.'

'Well, I saw Trevor visiting Kylie Cooper two days before he died,' Kathy said.

'What?' Sandra said, 'Why?'

'We don't know,' Miss Walsh said, 'He didn't say anything to you about her?'

'No, he didn't. But I'll tell you something, he weren't taking no drugs.'

'No, he wasn't,' Jan said, 'There were no drugs shown on the toxicology report during the post-mortem.'

'Maybe he were selling them?' Sandra said, her eyes round with horror. 'That's what he meant when he told Dan he were on to a good thing and would be getting lots of money to do up his tractors?'

'Kylie Cooper was on the playing field the morning your brother died as well,' Miss Walsh said, gently. 'She had one of Elizabeth's dogs with her, but when I saw her later, she denied ever having met me, and said she was allergic to dogs. There seems to be a link between Kylie and Trevor, but it may be coincidental; I don't know exactly. I have some other information about Kylie Cooper which I'll give to PC Rivers separately to this meeting and which might help find her and see if she had anything to do with Trevor's death.'

'D'you think she did then?' Sandra asked.

'It's possible,' Miss Walsh said, 'It just seems odd that she was on the playing field two days after he went to her house, and that he died that same morning. However, it was very foggy that morning, and it's entirely possible there was someone else on the field who I couldn't see. As I don't know exactly when Trevor was killed, it's possible that someone came on to the field after I left, but we do have to remember that Kylie Cooper found Trevor's body and rang the police.'

'Does that mean she didn't do it, then?' Sandra asked.

'Not necessarily; it's a well-known plot device in detective fiction,' Miss Walsh said, 'It diverts suspicion away from the person who discovered the body. Everyone assumes that the murderer wouldn't hang about or inform the police. It's also a good idea to pose as a dog-walker; think how many dead bodies dog walkers have found. Borrowing a dog from the Grange also confirms the link between Kylie Cooper and Angela Fawkes; it was definitely Durban who was with Kylie Cooper on the playing field that morning.'

'Durban is one of my dogs,' Elizabeth explained.

'It seems to me as though there is a line running from Amelia Frost to Angela Fawkes to Kylie Cooper and finally to Trevor Fish,' Miss Walsh said. 'And I do think if Trevor hadn't visited Kylie Cooper that night, he would still be alive.'

There was a silence as all the women thought through the information they'd heard so far, and Marjorie passed Sandra a box of tissues.

'I think that's it for now,' Miss Walsh said, 'I have a full report for PC Rivers, which contains all the information I've gathered about the drug selling in Tudlinghall, and I think we all deserve coffee and cake.'

She and Kathy went through to the kitchen, followed by Truncheon, who had learned that being near the counter where the cake was cut would often net him a bit from whoever was cutting it. Today proved to be no exception.

***

Later, as they drove to the school, and then walked down the playing field to the clearing, Miss Walsh filled Jan in with the other information she hadn't given out at the meeting.

'I managed to gain access to the house while Kylie Cooper was there, and saw trophies in a cabinet with the name 'H. Taylor' engraved on. When I Googled it, Helen Taylor was a former England Cricket player, and I saw her throwing a dog's ball very strongly when I met her as Kylie Cooper on the playing field,' Miss Walsh said. 'Did you find a cricket ball when you searched the playing field after Trevor's death?'

'No we didn't,' Jan said, and both women walked gingerly into the clearing, being very careful not to tread on any needles. 'Well, I'd say you've definitely found where they meet up. I'll get back to the station and let the DI know; he'll decide what to do.'

'When I was here taking the photograph,' Miss Walsh said, as she showed Jan how to navigate the pathway around the school field back to Church Plain, 'I overheard the young man saying that 'she' had gone, and he was now the main source for the drugs that the other young man wanted.'

'Right,' said Jan, 'Well, leave it up to us now, and thank you for your help.'

'Will you let me know if you find Kylie Cooper?' Miss Walsh asked a little hesitantly.

'I'll let you know what I can,' Jan said, 'But it probably won't be for some time.'

'I understand.'

With a new caretaker in place, Tudlinghall regained some serenity after the shock of Trevor's death. Miss Walsh saw Sandra a few times and learned that Trevor's house had been sold and on the advice of her solicitor, Sandra had sent Tish a cheque for exactly one quarter (once all fees and expenses had been deducted).

'And that were it,' Sandra said, with satisfaction, 'I han't heard from her again, and good riddance to bad rubbish, I say.'

'Well, at least she's not going to take you to court over this,' Miss Walsh said, 'That must be a great relief to you.'

'Oh I never thought she would,' Sandra said, 'She's a lazy cow.'

Marjorie's daughter bought the vacant house that Kylie Cooper had camped in, once the house agents had got the owners' permission to get a locksmith in to change the locks again. There was a lot of work to be done to get the house into a suitable condition, but Marjorie was having the time of her life helping her daughter choose paint colours, fabric, and utensils, and harrying workmen who were putting right all the structural problems.

All the children Miss Walsh had photographed were in the care of a charity which specialised in assisting young people to come off hard drugs, although the young man who'd been seen coming and going from Kylie Cooper's house seemed to have disappeared from the village as quietly as he'd arrived.

Kathy Berry won first prize in the cake competition at the Village Fete that summer, held for the first time after the Covid Lockdowns.

The school was greatly relieved that they no longer had to litter-pick the field for needles and drug-taking paraphernalia before the children could go out to play. One-use-plastic litter remained a huge problem for the entire village, and Miss Walsh set up a weekly litter-picking group to tackle it.

Both Elizabeth and Miss Walsh (separately) cashed in their offer of a free week's house and dog-sitting from 'Home First'; Elizabeth went out to

Portugal with her son and daughter-in-law and their two children. While Miss Walsh went to London and enjoyed being a tourist around all the sights, and having treatments in a luxury spa hotel. Truncheon was spoiled rotten by the house-sitter, and had to be put on a diet when his mistress returned home.

And so a whole year passed by in normal innocent village activities, and Miss Walsh had almost forgotten about Trevor Fish and Kylie Cooper, when she found a police car parked on her drive-way as she returned from another of the very long walkies intended to slim Truncheon back down to the svelte ex-police dog he had once been.

PC Jan Rivers got out of the car, and Miss Walsh greeted her with enthusiasm.

'Hello! How nice to see you, do come in.'

Jan declined any refreshments, saying she only had a moment, and was here unofficially anyway.

'So, have you found Kylie Cooper?' Miss Walsh asked, 'Or should I say, Helen Taylor?'

'All I can tell you is that, as far as we know, the drugs ring we believe to have been set-up in Tudlinghall has been completely dismantled, and all those involved are being dealt with by the appropriate agencies.'

'And did you look into the link between the house-sitting and the drug rings?'

'Some enquiries are still on-going,' Jan said, and then added a little hesitantly, 'You know that there is some, shall I say, opposition to your involvement in cases?'

Miss Walsh nodded; oh yes, she knew all right!

'So, I hope you'll understand when I say that I can't tell you anymore; but that off the record, I believe we wouldn't have got this far without your help?'

Miss Walsh nodded again. Jan hesitated, and then said, 'Completely off the record?' looking very hard at Miss Walsh.

'You have my word,' she said.

'Then yes, we've made that link, and yes we've caught Helen Taylor and proved that she's been masquerading as Kelly and Kylie Cooper. We believe she murdered Amelia Frost. We haven't caught Angela Fawkes, though, and Helen Taylor won't tell us who she is, or where we can find her, not even for a reduced prison sentence.'

'Might that suggest a closer relationship than a working one?' Miss Walsh suggested. 'Did Helen Taylor have any children?'

'Enquiries are on-going,' Jan said, clearly back on the record again.

There was a pause as they looked at each other, but Miss Walsh could tell that the police hadn't thought to follow that line of enquiry.

'And the young man who she brought in to Mattishall to help her get the drugs to the kids?' she asked.

'Yes, we have found him, and he's in the care of the local authorities,' Jan said.

'And Trevor Fish?' Miss Walsh asked, but Jan shook her head.

'The Coroner's verdict stands,' she said, 'Death was an accident.'

'Well, thank you for coming to update me,' Miss Walsh said, 'Please give my regards to DC Whitaker.'

'I will,' Jan said, and made a bit of a fuss of Truncheon before she left. 'Is it my imagination, or has he put on a bit of weight?' she asked.

WHAT ACTUALLY HAPPENED - TREVOR IS THE ARCHITECT OF HIS OWN DOOM

'Them kids are back!' Mandy called from the bar.

'I'll send them packing,' Trevor called back, but as he approached the open window next to the door, he heard their voices and there was something about them which made him pause, and listen.

'C'mon man,' one of them was saying in a whiny desperate voice, 'I need some!'

'Got cash?' the other one said.

'No.'

'Well, I can't just give it you, can I?' the second voice said, reasonably. 'It costs me to get it, and then I pass the cost on to my lucky customers.'

'You give it me before,' the first voice said sulkily.

'That was a taster, to see if you liked it,' the second voice said, still reasonably, 'I can't go on giving it away, or I won't make any money, will I?'

'I guess not. But I told you I haven't got any money. I've already sold my phone,' the first voice said, on a rising note of desperation.

'Well, there is a way you can earn some if you want,' the second voice said, in a considering tone.

'How? I'll do anything.'

'I know someone nearby, she'll give you two hundred pound to get you going.'

'Why would she do that?'

'To help you look street, like me, so you can get punters of your own. Look at these, and this, pretty sick, huh?'

'Yeah, but what do I have to do in return? '

'Nothing much. You just sell stuff, give her a bit back, and buy some more stuff off of her to sell. It's a business, see?'

'So … all I have to do is sell the stuff?'

'Yeah, and you can then buy as much as you want for yourself.'

By now the listening man was as hooked as the hapless teenage boy. All thoughts of sending them packing were gone, and he was forming a plan in his own mind. A business proposition to put to this entrepreneurial woman; one that would benefit them both.

'All right,' the first boy said, 'I'll do it! When can I get the money? And the stuff to sell, and some for me?' There was such eagerness in his voice that the listening man winced a bit. You got to be a bit harder than that my man, he thought, it don't do to appear too eager.

'Follow me, my son,' the second voice said, with the unmistakeable triumph of a Fagin persuading Oliver Twist to pick a pocket or two, 'I'll lead you right to fame and fortune, you've made a wise choice.'

When the boys moved off around the side of the building, the man slipped out through the door and cautiously tailed them. They weren't expecting anyone to be following them and didn't look around as they left the car-park and headed across the road. There was no street lighting, but it wasn't particularly dark and the man could see the two boys were in their mid to late teens, and had he known anything about teen fashion, he'd have realised that one was dressed in expensive designer clothes and shoes, and the other one wasn't.

They didn't go far down the road, just to a small bungalow, where one boy knocked on a door and both stepped in when it opened.

Trevor stood in some shadows and waited for the boys to re-emerge. They were in there quite a while, but eventually came out, one congratulating the other on joining up, while the other was too busy counting notes to respond, and they walked off together towards the village without noticing him.

He strode up to the door and knocked.

A woman in her late middle-age opened the door to see a man standing there.

'I over-heard them kids talking; you're peddling drugs to kids,' he said.

'I have no idea what you are talking about,' she said, and went to close the door again, but he put his hand hard against the door, pushing it back at her.

'I think you better let me in,' he said, 'Or I'm calling the cops.'

She shrugged, but stood back and let him in, peering out into the driveway as she did so; there was no-one else about.

'What do you want?' she asked.

'Money, of course,' he said.

'Or what?'

'Or I go to the police and tell them about you.'

'How much?'

'Two thousand to start with.'

'I don't have that sort of money in the house.'

'You give that boy two hundred.'

'So? I tell you I don't keep that sort of money in the house.'

'When can you get it?'

'Tomorrow?'

'All right,' he said, 'I'll give you till Friday; that's an extra day. Come to the playing field at seven in the morning. I'll be there waiting. You don't show, you don't bring the money in cash, I'm calling the cops.'

The man left, and the woman was straight on the phone.

'Those stupid boys were overheard.'

'How? Who by?'

'I don't know who he is, but he says he overheard them and came to the house after they'd gone.'

'Right. Get up here now, and I'll tell you what to do.'

The woman made her way up to Tudlinghall Grange in the dark, and her contact was waiting for her at the kitchen door. There was a gun on the table.

'You'll have to put him out of the way.'

The dogs had stood up and were stretching, the younger one started scratching at the back door to be let out. The woman opened the door and he bounded out into the dark, while the older dog settled back down in her basket with a deep sigh.

'When and where does he want the money?'

'Friday seven am on the playing field.'

'Right, come here first, take one of the dogs and you can pretend to be a dog walker. Shoot him, bring the dog and the gun back here, go back to the field and ring it in to the police, then sit tight, there's nothing to link you to him. Give it a few weeks, wrap up your business here, then get out of Tudlinghall. Now you've mopped up that little matter in Peterborough, there's nothing to keep you here.'

On Friday morning, the woman collected the younger dog and walked down the road to the playing field. It was thick fog, but she could see vague shape of the man standing a short way down the field. As she approached, he walked away from her across the field towards a tractor, which was already running, belching exhaust fumes which mingled with the fog. The dog pulled the lead out of her hand and went prancing off, another dog chased it back again: there was someone else on the field. She couldn't shoot him while there was someone else about. She cursed as she started walking down the field following the man and wondering what the hell he was playing at. Why wasn't he standing still waiting for her to bring him his money?

The dogs dashed up and off again, the man climbed aboard the tractor then started to drive away slowly down the field. She didn't have much time. She put her hand in her pocket and discovered a cricket ball. A left-over from her glory days. She hefted the ball in her hand, aimed, and threw.

She heard a thump and walked in the direction she'd thrown the ball. It was there on the ground, and the tractor was trundling off towards the boundary; the man was slumped sideways in the seat. She picked the ball up and stowed it back in her pocket.

Belatedly she realised she didn't know what the damn dog was called, and so she stumbled about the field calling the only dog name she could think of, and heard an answering shout. The owner of the other dog had caught the lead and handed it back to her. She did her best to behave like a normal dog-walker, throwing balls for the animal until the other woman left.

Then she took the dog and the gun back to her contact.

'I couldn't use this,' she said, putting the gun down on the kitchen table, 'There were other people on the field.'

The dog settled back in its basket with a sigh and fell asleep.

'So what did you do?' her contact asked.

'I threw a cricket ball and hit him on the back of his head,' she said, pulling the ball out of her pocket and looking thoughtfully at it. 'That will have knocked him out at least, maybe even broken his skull.'

'You'd better get back there and make sure he's dead,' her contact said, stowing the gun away safely. 'If he's not, then improvise. We're nearly done here; we don't want him calling the cops.'

She returned to the playing field. There didn't seem to be anyone about.

The tractor had toppled over into a ditch, the man was trapped underneath, not moving: she took a deep breath, and dialled 999.

THE MAIN POINTS OF MISS WALSH'S REPORT TO THE POLICE:

1. Amelia Frost - That Mrs Harte's usual house-sitter was substituted without the agency knowing. Then she was murdered. Prior to her death, she was in contact with a woman called 'Kelly or Kylie Cooper' purportedly from an agency called 'Mi Casa, Tu Casa', who offered her a job in Spain – possibly getting her out of the way so that a substitute house-sitter could be installed in her place.

2. The substitute house-sitter was called 'Angela Fawkes'; Mrs Harte said she was a younger woman, probably in her 30s, and looked after the house and dogs very well. Miss Walsh believes there to be a connection between these two events – Kelly/Kylie Cooper and Angela Fawkes were both in Tudlinghall at the same time, but she never saw them together, nor did she witness Kelly/Kyle visiting Tudlinghall Hall, nor Angela visiting Kelly/Kylie.

3. Kylie Cooper – she appeared to have cuckooed a house on West Green. It was on the market, and she may have applied to see around it, and then changed the locks. She almost certainly removed the 'For Sale' sign to discourage interest in the property. She didn't engage with neighbours at all if she could help it. Miss Walsh met her on the playing field on the morning of Trevor's death, and she was with a dog she called 'Bella', which was male. Later she denied having met Miss Walsh, and said she was allergic to dogs. Miss Berry saw lots of young people coming and going from Kylie's house, and also saw Trevor visit her, two days before he died.

4. The dog 'Bella' was actually 'Durban' a male Golden Retriever owned by Mrs Harte at Tudlinghall Hall – and Angela was house-sitting at Tudlinghall Hall when Trevor was killed - thus providing a link between Angela and Kylie. Why would Kylie be walking a stranger's dog, especially if she was allergic to them? She has to have known Angela prior to arriving at Tudlinghall.

5. Miss Berry identified two young men as having been at Kylie Cooper's house from a photograph taken by Miss Walsh of young people around a fire at the back of the school playing field, where drug paraphernalia was

found on a daily basis. Miss Walsh overheard their conversation about a woman who was no longer in Tudlinghall, leaving one of the young men as the main contact for obtaining drugs, and the other had been drawn in to selling drugs by becoming addicted.

6. Miss Walsh believes that Kylie Cooper is actually Helen Taylor, a former England Cricket player – and witnessed her throwing a ball very strongly. She had cricket trophies with the name 'H Taylor' engraved on in her sitting room. The only reason to change her name and be anti-social is that she is up to No Good.

7. It appears that Kylie Cooper and Angela Fawkes have manoeuvred themselves into Tudlinghall in order to set up a drug-dealing business and recruit young people as pushers.

8. However, the fact that Trevor also visited Kylie Cooper two days before his death suggests a link between the two, as does the fact that Kylie was on the playing field on the day of Trevor's death, and that she lied subsequently about having met Miss Walsh there.

9. 'Discovering' the body, is a well-known ruse for making people assume she has nothing to do with the death, backed up by the fact that Kylie was posing as a dog-walker; dog-walkers are constantly tripping over bodies ... it appears she borrowed the dog to give her a reason to be on the field that morning – linking her with Angela Fawkes.

10. According to Sandra, Trevor had told his brother-in-law that he was on to something which would bring him in a lot of money – if he was attempting to blackmail Kylie about the drug-dealing, she might have killed him, or arranged for someone else (Angela?) to kill him. However, the only person Miss Walsh saw on the playing field that morning was Kylie. But, (a) it was thick fog, (b) Miss Walsh doesn't know exactly when Trevor was killed, so it might have been after Kylie left the field, (c) Angela was staying at Tudlinghall Hall which borders the playing field ...

All four are linked – Amelia Frost – Angela Fawkes – Kylie Cooper – Trevor Fish ...

Printed in Great Britain
by Amazon